L'Chaim and Lamentations

L'Chaim and Lamentations

Stories by

CRAIG DARCH

NewSouth Books

Montgomery

NewSouth Books
105 S. Court Street
Montgomery, AL 36104

Library of Congress Cataloging-in-Publication Data

Names: Darch, Craig B., author.
Title: L'chaim and lamentations : stories / by Craig Darch.
Description: Montgomery : NewSouth Books, [2019].
Identifiers: LCCN 2018042901 (print) | LCCN 2018059221 (ebook) |
 ISBN 9781588383709 (Ebook) | ISBN 9781588383693 (hardcover)
Subjects: LCSH: Short stories, Jewish.
Classification: LCC PS3604.A7248 (ebook) | LCC PS3604.A7248 A6
2018
 (print) | DDC 813/.6--dc23
LC record available at https://lccn.loc.gov/2018042901

Design by Randall Williams

Printed in the United States of America

ACKNOWLEDGMENTS

I want to thank Suzanne La Rosa and Randall Williams of
NewSouth Books for their enthusiastic support and careful guid-
ance through each phase of the publication process. Thanks also
to Beth Marino for editing the book; her suggestions regarding
style made the book much better. She is a joy to work with. My
brothers, Mike and Lance, and my sister, Debbie, took an active
interest in the book and were a source of great support. Finally,
I want to thank my wife, Gabriele, and my son, Eric, for their
love and encouragement. They are the best.

To my parents,
Dorothy and Will Darch,
who loved Jewish books
and loved each other

Contents

Acknowledgments / 4

Glossary / 8

Sadie's Prayer / 9

Wasserman's Ride Home / 27

Kaddish for Two / 44

Leonard Saperstein & Company / 66

The Last Jew in Krotoszyn / 90

Who's the Old Crone? / 117

Miss Bargman / 145

Glossary

Kapos: prisoners in a Nazi concentration camp who served as guards or supervisors of other prisoners

l'chaim: a toast—to life!

mishigas: craziness

pupik: bellybutton

puppele: term of endearment—little doll

Rashi: Rabbi Shlomo Yitzchaki (French, 1040–1105); famous Biblical scholar and author

shmatte: a rag-like or shabby item of clothing

Sadie's Prayer

~~~~~~~~~~~~~~~~

From her warm bed, Esther shuddered when she heard the clattering of a coffee cup placed onto a saucer. She couldn't help but think of the mess that always accompanied Sadie and fret over the growing pile of cake crumbs and the collection of crumpled napkins she knew would be strewn around the gray formica-topped kitchen table, not to mention the swirling cigarette smoke from Sadie's ever-present Lucky Strike. Sadie is such a slob, she thought bitterly, while turning her head from side to side to loosen her stiff neck. That half-wit must have been up most of the night again smoking and reading those communist books of hers. "Ach," she snorted, "I'm not even out of bed yet and already that Sadie Moskowitz is rubbing my nerves raw."

She pushed her woolen blanket to one side and slowly sat up, putting both feet on the cold wood floor. Her misshapen feet ached, but the dull pain faded as she remembered Sadie. Of all the roommates! I get stuck with an anarchist, a seventy-nine-year-old rabble-rouser. It's a miracle the FBI hasn't come to investigate what goes on here. I'm just one raid away from jail. And I can thank that miserable housing agency—a Jewish one no less. Why would they match such opposites? She glared at Sadie's side of the room: the unmade bed with stacks of newspapers and magazines encircling it like a moat, the piles of clothes strewn on the floor, the gloomy poster darkening the whole room. Esther turned to gaze instead at her deceased husband, smiling from a framed photograph on her nightstand. "Oy, Max," she groaned, "where are you when I need you? You must be rolling over in your grave knowing how things have turned out for me."

Esther slipped on her white terry cloth robe and tied it tightly around her thin waist, took hold of her aluminum walker, shuffled across the room, breathed deeply, braced herself, and opened the bedroom door.

"Well, there she is already! It's sleeping beauty herself," cried Sadie Moskowitz, enthroned in her seat at the kitchen table. "Come sit with Sadie and have your cake and coffee. I'll even serve you this morning—proving I don't take serious your insults from last night."

Through the haze of cigarette smoke, Esther saw the crumbs from Sadie's breakfast scattered across the table and over the worn linoleum floor and spied a book emblazoned with the title, *Workers Revolt!*

Disgusted, Esther shook her head, waved the smoke away, and snorted, "Ach, another time I have to hear about workers' rights? What about my rights? All these months living with you and every morning it's communist books and crumb cake. With my Max it was always the *Forward* and lox and bagels. Every morning for forty years it was the *Forward* and lox and bagels."

"If you haven't noticed, Esther, your Max is reading the newspaper and having his bagels someplace else this morning," Sadie said dismissively. "Entenmann's crumb cake with Sadie Moskowitz—that, my bourgeois friend, will just have to do." She gestured to the chair across the table. "Here, sit. Don't kvetch so much about your breakfast. I have been eating Entenmann's over seventy years. It contains all the nutrients you need for normal activity. What, my ornery friend is planning on digging ditches this morning?"

Ignoring Sadie, Esther shivered, rubbed her bony arms vigorously, and moaned, "Again this morning that miser Stein has cut the heat. It's a meat locker in here. May he and that numbskull wife of his rot in their heated apartment."

"Enough already, Esther, with the death wishes. And this from the pious one who believes in You-Know-Who."

"Don't tell me *enough*. And I've told you, stop with the You-Know-Who business. It's a dangerous thing to talk like a heretic. Anyway, I've been inside Stein's apartment. It's the Bahamas in there. And in here we get Siberia." Esther's breathing suddenly became erratic; she placed both hands on her chest and took several deep breaths to calm herself.

"Esther, relax or it will be the hyperventilation again. I'll talk to Stein and remind him the two flowers in the Garden of Eden need just a little heat to bloom." She slid a piping hot cup of coffee toward Esther. "Here, this will warm you. Anyway, it's not just Stein, it's your poor circulation; that's why you're always cold. You need to be more active like me, not sit on your *tuchas* so much . . ."

"It's not my circulation," cried Esther. "Not enough activity? And this coming from Sadie Moskowitz, the Queen of Sheba, who doesn't even lift her little finger around here. I'll give you activity. Just who do you think keeps this apartment clean? And who, may I ask, puts dinner on the table on a budget of pennies? Ach, I can't win with you. That cheapskate Stein turns down the heat and when I freeze you accuse me of poor circulation. What, now the know-it-all Sadie Moskowitz is a doctor?"

Esther pushed her walker to the side and lowered herself into a kitchen chair, crossed her legs, and shook her head as she watched Sadie slice a thin piece of coffee cake.

"Why such a small piece of Entenmann's?" screeched Esther. "Who can live on such a tiny portion? I've hardly the strength to lift my fork. What, you're trying to send me to my grave? And, may I ask, were you so stingy with yourself this morning? Am I the one to suffer because of our financial predicament, an eighty-year-old widow? A stingy rabble-rouser, that's what you are." As she spoke, Esther brushed the cake crumbs on her side of the table into a neat pile with her stiff, blue-veined hand.

"There is no winning with you," countered Sadie. "First you don't want coffee cake—only lox and bagels are good enough for Miss Fancy Pants. Now, after all your complaining, you want a bigger piece. Your Max must have suffered two lifetimes from your meshuga behavior.

The poor man must have pleaded with You-Know-Who for an early departure and then danced to his grave for a little peace."

"You leave my Max out of this. You're nothing but a communist and a heretic," spat Esther, her taut face twisted with anger.

Both sat stiffly and eyed each other warily across the table.

Sadie finally broke the impasse, "Let's not quarrel. For once, let's be civil to one another . . . So Esther, did you sleep last night?"

"Who can sleep in such a place? Like a lunatic you're up all night making noise and filling everywhere with smoke. From the aggravation my heart palpitations get worse by the second. It's no wonder I'm always on the verge of collapse. It's just a matter of seconds before I'm rushed to the hospital and put on cardiac life support. It will be a gift from God if I live out the day."

Impervious, Sadie cried raspily, "Not slept? I looked in on you. Like a corpse you were. Not once did you move, just wheezing and snoring the whole night. Such sleep should happen to me. Anyway, my testy friend who thinks she will exit this world in a matter of seconds, for your information, do you know that today we celebrate our anniversary?"

"Anniversary? What, Max and I have an anniversary?" Esther asked, her eyes suddenly vacant.

"No, Esther, your Max is dead for twenty years, remember? Again, it's one of your thinking spells, and so early in the morning. It's *our* anniversary. It's to the day one year since we are roommates."

"One year? It feels like forty years wandering in the desert." Esther raised her eyes, clear and lively again, to the ceiling and groaned, "Oy, Max, how much longer do I have to suffer till I join you?"

Sadie waved dismissively at Esther. "For once leave your Max alone. Why spoil his peaceful breakfast? Anyway, what do you know about suffering? Sadie Moskowitz's education was the sweat shops and the picket lines in Brooklyn. For everything in my life I had to suffer. You were one of those fancy Barnard girls; everything was handed to you on a silver platter . . ."

"Oy, don't remind me," Esther sighed. "Those days are long gone. I can't tell you how I miss my life: the candle-lit dinners and dancing with my Max, every afternoon mah-jongg with the girls . . . Now look at me. All I have to my name are memories of my Max, a communist roommate making terrible plots, and more tsuris than Job. I'm tell-ing you, old age has been a curse for me, Sadie. Each day begins lousy with aches and pains and ends even worse. Every night I ask God, who I know from personal experi-ence happens to be hard of hearing, for what sins am I being punished? And, like always, never do I get so much as a hint, much less an answer. I can't tell you how lonely the nights are without my Max."

"Memories shmemories. Stop so much with the memories. I'm up to my *pupik* with your memories. Lonely nights? Sadie Moskowitz could write a book on cold, lonely nights." She sighed wistfully. "Ah, but when I was young, it was different. I rarely wasted a night. Tell me, Esther, back then were you enthusiastic, too?"

"What enthusiastic? Again you talk goofy. Who can understand what you mean?"

"I mean with your Max. Were you enthusiastic in bed, you know, when he . . ."

"Such a thing to ask, and before lunch even!" choked Esther, her face flushed. "I never heard such talk in my life. The questions you ask. I would never think of my Max in that way; never. No lady would. I was taught not to talk about such things."

"It's not healthy, Esther, to keep everything bottled up inside. It's a proven fact—such a thing can cause dangerous blockages in your system. That may be the source of your palpitations. Anyway, I was taught to speak my mind, and between you and me, Esther, I was enthusiastic with all my partners, every one of them. I tried to list them one night when I couldn't sleep." She leaned forward, displaying a gleam in her eye and a row of shiny, white false teeth, and whispered across the table, "Esther, there were more than I could remember . . ."

"Oy vey," Esther cried. "Such shenanigans I have to hear about this morning, in my own apartment even."

Sadie, oblivious to Esther's protests, continued, "I can't say any one of them was better than the next, at least from what I can remember . . . well, maybe Manny. He was what you might call . . . gifted. Oh, how I loved being the center of his attentions. But Manny was like all the union men in those days; the only time a woman got his attention was in the bedroom. At the union hall women weren't respected; it was always, 'make a snack,' or 'clean up.' Always the men in charge, and Manny was the worst, constantly barking orders. I learned no man wants to share the spotlight. That's why I gave Manny his pink slip and dropped him like a hot knish. I asked myself, does Sadie Moskowitz need such tsuris just for the privilege of a few minutes under the wedding canopy?"

"Well," countered Esther, "did you ever consider maybe a spotlight should shine on only one person at a time?"

"But why should it always shine on the man? Anyway, my satisfied homemaker, what did marriage ever give you?"

"It gave me forty years of happiness with my Max, and for me that was enough. Now look what you did," Esther moaned, shaking her head. "You got me thinking about my Max again. Oy, how I still miss him. I can't believe it's been over twenty years since I buried my Max. Such a life! I can't remember from one second to the next, but I remember that day like it was yesterday because that day I died, too." She scooped up the last few crumbs on her plate and licked her fork clean.

"For someone so dead, Esther, you sure eat your fill of coffee cake."

"Ach, who can in this apartment have a normal conversation? It's always the kibitzing with you, Sadie . . ."

"Okay, okay, I'm sorry." Sadie leaned across the table. "Tell me, Sadie Moskowitz is all ears. What do you remember about that day?"

"Oy, do I remember! You've never seen such a funeral. So many came, even some of Max's old employees. And you should have heard the stories they told about my Max. I'll never forget them, no matter how bad my memory gets. Rabbi Cohen said if Max hadn't lost everything in the Depression, he would have made a name for himself. Those were the rabbi's exact words. And now look at what's happened to me. Every day I sit in a shabby godforsaken apartment with a communist plotting who knows what kind of subversion," she snapped as she drained the last swallow of coffee from her cup.

"Again, Esther, it's the communist accusations with you. You're as bad as that half-wit McCarthy was. But, because it's our anniversary, I'll ignore your insults. Anyway, I can tell you a thing or two about funerals. Sadie Moskowitz has attended her share. My last one was Manny's. I hadn't seen him in years, but one day I saw his obituary in the *Times*. He finagled his way to the top and had some fancy schmancy job in the Garment Union. Ach, when I think of the three years of my life I wasted with that no-goodnik, the miserable two-timer. And this, may I add, from the son of a rabbi from the old country, no less. I could tell you such things, Esther, about that womanizer. Anyway, all his girlfriends showed up. I think they wanted the satisfaction of seeing him in his grave. You've never seen such a joyous occasion. All the girlfriends left the cemetery beaming. I even heard a few mazel tovs on the way out. You'd have thought it was a bar mitzvah! Such a meshug-gener that man was. All those years Manny lecturing me about liberating the worker and equal opportunity—I didn't know he meant equal opportunity for him to sleep with every woman he met . . ."

"Well, my Max was different. I never had a moment's worry about such things," Esther gloated.

"Ach, like always, it's all about your Max." Sadie lit a Lucky Strike, inhaled deeply, blew out a stream of smoke and began, "Your Max . . ."

Esther, suddenly preoccupied, didn't hear her roommate. She was twisting the wedding band on her finger. From the tangle of memories about Max, one pulls her away, and she finds herself standing in her apartment on Prospect Street waiting for him. The dinner table is beautifully set for his arrival. A silver tureen of hot matzo ball soup sits in the middle of the table next to a bowl of chopped liver; a mountain of sliced onions are heaped on a dish. A tender brisket made juicy and caramel-sweet by her secret ingredient, Coca-Cola, simmers in a pot on the counter, ready for serving. Two crystal wine glasses, filled to their brims, shimmer in the light. Suddenly there is a noise at the front door, and Max comes in and plops his camel hair overcoat and fedora on a chair. Without a word, Max takes her into his arms, and Esther squeezes back with all her might . . .

As though in a dream, more memories of Max rush at her. It's a wintry morning in Brooklyn. She and Max are strolling hand in hand down Pitkin Avenue. A frosty wind swirls around them and bites their faces. Icy snowflakes cover everything with a crusty, white blanket. "Let's stop at

Grabstein's for a pickled tongue on rye and an egg cream,"
she says, pressing herself against him to get warm . . .

" . . . Esther, are you listening to me?" Sadie called impatiently. "You didn't hear a word I said. Again it's the
thinking spells. What am I going to do with you?"

Esther was still trembling with thoughts of her Max,
and she could still feel the cold sting of the wind and snow
on her hollow cheeks and the lingering taste of pickled
tongue on rye in her mouth.

"Ach, what's to hear?" Esther spat. "Lectures by the
heretic, Lefty Moskowitz."

"Oy vey, now I'm Lefty Moskowitz! It's one insult after
another with you, Esther. But you're wrong about that
heretic business. A heretic doesn't believe in You-Know-
Who—I'm just not sure; the jury is still out. For this I
need concrete proof, like a corned beef sandwich sitting
in front of me. I see, I eat, I believe."

"I hate to be the one to remind you, Sadie, but at your
advanced age you don't have much more time to settle ac-
counts. But how can you if you don't pray once in a while?"

"About that, Esther, you're wrong. Sadie Moskowitz
in her lifetime has done her share of praying. After I left
that two-timer Manny, I prayed for him a heart attack.
Oy, the praying I did. Everyday at the crack of dawn, like
I was saying the morning blessings, I prayed. After lunch
I whispered sweet prayers for revenge, and I prayed on
picket lines holding protest signs—you try picketing and
praying at the same time without hurting yourself, it's

not easy. Even on my knees before bed I prayed for that womanizer to experience chest pains. Like a rabbi I was for all my praying. Nobody on this earth prayed like Sadie Moskowitz prayed. I even gave You-Know-Who advice on the time and place to finish Manny off in case He was not so good with details and needed just a little nudge. And what did Sadie Moskowitz, the pious one, get for her trouble? I'll tell you what I got. Bupkes, I got! Until his heart attack *fifty years* later. And I ask you, Esther, this kind of service is proof?"

"You think just because you prayed once in a while you should get immediate action? For you it should be different than any other Jew? Ach, just look at me, I'm sitting with the eminent Rabbi Moskowitz who thinks she should have a direct line to God. If you haven't noticed already, Jews are chosen to be put on hold." Esther shook her head. "So, these are my golden years? For the short time I have left, I'm condemned to sit with a communist who prays for heart attacks. Huh, for me not one year has been golden, not one! Who could know getting old would bring such tsuris? This life is a curse."

"Esther, for once you're right. But don't think you've cornered the market on *tsuris*. Getting old has not exactly been a stroll in paradise for Sadie Moskowitz, either. It's just one day, the same day, over and over. And to top that, at night I just lie there, awake. I can't tell you the strange things that race through my mind late at night. I lie there thinking and shrinking. I am getting shorter by the day! How can a person shrink? And not only that, every day my life gets smaller and smaller, just the four walls of this jail cell. This isn't a life, it's a death sentence! What I wouldn't give for something fun to break the monotony."

"Something fun? What, at your age you should have a party?" snorted Esther.

"Yes!" cried Sadie, her eyes at once lively behind her thick glasses. "Finally, Esther, you have a good idea! Yes, why not a party? Esther, Sadie Moskowitz has just decided. Today we will spend preparing for our anniversary celebration. And for such an occasion we must have something special for our dinner." Sadie thought for a moment, her forehead wrinkling, then said with wet lips, "Esther, it's been ages since you made your famous matzo ball soup. Can we have it tonight?"

Esther raised her gray eyebrows as she considered Sadie's request. Then she shrugged her narrow, stooped shoulders and said, "For once you ask nice. So, if it's matzo ball soup you want, I'll prepare matzo ball soup."

"Can you make the matzo balls small and crispy like last time?" Sadie added, an expectant smile lighting her face.

"Ach, why not? If it's crispy you want, I'll make crispy. But I need to stop at Karp's and pick up matzo meal, carrots, and chicken—and more prune juice; I'm suffering from the constipation again." She grimaced as she rubbed her stomach. "So, I'm warning you, Sadie, don't rush me like always."

Straightening in her seat so she was eye level with Sadie, Esther said with authority, "Now it's Esther Hirsh who's making a decision. So just listen for the first time ever: we'll eat off mother's white linen and light candles and say the blessings. So maybe for once you can eat like a normal human being and not spill all over the place. And another thing, for the occasion, we'll dress nice, not the *shmattes* we usually wear." Her voice turned energetic, girlish. "And maybe even listen to some nice music, not the TV blaring like always."

"To have the pleasure of sipping your delicious matzo ball soup, Esther, I'll do anything you ask. And I'll even pick up a bottle of Manischewitz. We can have with our soup a glass of wine to celebrate our anniversary."

"For an anniversary such as ours," Esther sighed, "maybe the whole bottle will be necessary." She rose stiffly and reached to gather the cups and saucers as she did each morning, but Sadie nudged her away, collected the breakfast dishes into a neat stack, and said, "Go get dressed already. I'll clean up. Save your energy for the soup. You'll soon understand, Esther, you need a friend like me; you need Sadie Moskowitz."

"Like a pestilence I need you," Esther half smiled and slowly turned and shuffled off, her noisy walker leading the way.

A nervous grimace passed across her face as she worried whether she'd remember, once there, why she had gone to the bedroom in the first place. After a few more steps, she paused to catch her breath and, like an exhausted marathon runner, surveyed the distance to the bedroom. She groaned, closing her eyes. At once, it is 1925, a redolent spring evening, her beloved Max, young and dashing, whirls her across a ballroom floor to the rhythm of Benny Goodman's band, her white chiffon dress billowing with each turn. She feels weightless in Max's arms, and her feet barely touch the gleaming parquet floor.

Then, in mid-song, the music is gone as quickly as one of Max's soft, unexpected kisses. The aroma of perfume is replaced by the musty smell of the shabby apartment. But before the inevitable longing took hold, Esther reassured herself that it would not be long before she would join Max and finish that dance, and once again everything would be just right.

"Esther, Esther," Sadie's booming voice filled the tiny apartment. "There you go again, daydreaming about Max, like always. I can tell by that faraway look . . ."

"Ach, now, among other things, the great Sadie Moskowitz is a mind reader," Esther scoffed, her eyes as soft as if she'd just awakened from a dream. She entered the bedroom and immediately tensed as she caught sight of the poster over Sadie's bed: the burning, predatory gaze of Karl Marx, his bushy gray beard and thick coarse hair framing a large, round face, his coal-black eyes following her around the room through the dust and shadows. Esther flinched under his exacting gaze and called out sharply to Sadie, "Every morning I have to be greeted by that communist and hear such talk from you, such meshuga talk. This I have to look forward to for the short time I have left on this earth."

"Enough about Karl Marx, Esther. Such complaining

causes wrinkles. Besides, you had your Max, let me have my Marx. Now get ready, or we'll never get out of this godforsaken apartment."

Esther shook her head, muttered out of the corner of her mouth about having to spend the rest of her life with a communist, and closed the bedroom door.

Sadie stood motionless for several moments and listened to the faint sounds of Esther dressing. She sighed and placed the cups and saucers into the sink. With two well-aimed swipes of her pudgy hand, she deftly brushed the cake crumbs from the table onto the floor and shrugged. So who will see? Anyway, Esther will sweep it up later; that girl loves to clean. And the activity will be good for her circulation. She leaned against the kitchen counter and thought of their anniversary celebration—finally, something to look forward to. She cocked her head to listen for sounds from the bedroom, but there was only silence.

Sadie called impatiently to the closed door, "Esther, come on already and stop the daydreaming. We're not getting any younger. Let's get out of here before You-Know-Who finds a reason to ruin our plans. And to show you Sadie Moskowitz is not a cheapskate, lunch will be my treat. Wear that blue turtleneck and bundle up. You could catch your death waiting for that bus of ours that's always late." Knowing Esther's dislike for being rushed, she added, "Just remember, Esther, before you get mad at me like always, you need a friend like Sadie Moskowitz."

Sadie tiptoed to a dusty table piled high with her books, carefully selected one from the bottom of the stack, opened it, and drew twenty dollars from the middle pages. Convinced that would be enough for lunch and a nice bottle of Manischewitz, she kissed the book as though it was a sacred text and returned it to its place.

Suddenly, she was overcome with excitement about their day, but Sadie knew the feeling would last only a moment before worry about her Esther nagged again. She waved away a twinge of melancholy already beginning to burrow deep into her chest. Then she raised her face upward and, with half-closed eyes, spoke just loud enough to gain the attention of the Hard-of-Hearing-One:

"I'm not praying, mind you, because I'm not so sure I even believe in such with the *mishigas* and tsuris me and Esther have suffered in our lives. But just in case, maybe it's not too much to ask this one time that You should not forget about Sadie Moskowitz and Esther Hirsh who live in Brooklyn on Fulton Avenue in Apartment 2E, and give us a few more good years without Esther's thinking spells getting worse, and, if I can be blunt, finagle a little heat from that weasel Stein before I wring his neck. If you haven't noticed already, Esther suffers terrible palpitations from the cold, as well as nervousness, headaches, indigestion accompanied by terrible gas, and frequent moodiness. And, by the way, just so You understand Sadie Moskowitz just a little, Esther thinks You're hard of hearing, but do You know what I think? I think You hear exactly what You want to hear. So just in case You're listening, I must ask one more thing. When the time comes for Esther to join her Max, could You make it my time, too, and ask them to save just a little room for me? Because even up there with You and her Max, with all her peculiarities, Esther will need a friend like Sadie Moskowitz."

She sighed heavily from her effort. Her razor-sharp eyes became soft and dreamy and momentarily fell on the bedroom door. Then Sadie Moskowitz hurried to the closet, pulled out their winter coats, took her place at the kitchen table, and gently fluffed the thick fur of Esther's collar as she waited for her friend.

Wasserman's Ride Home

"Thank God, finally an empty one," Ira Wasserman muttered, his thin voice barely audible in the deserted subway station. Crowded trains were something the seventy-three-year-old Wasserman avoided. For the first time that week something had gone his way.

Just maybe now I can find for myself a little peace and quiet, Wasserman thought, as the train rolled to a halt.

Wasserman stepped cautiously into the car and looked from one end to the other, making sure it was indeed empty. One could not be too cautious. Reassured, Wasserman groaned and, with the greatest care, wiped clean with his hands the grimy bench, then slid heavily into the seat he always took, the one up front near the door facing the windows directly across the aisle. From this perch he could not only observe the entire car, but more importantly see anyone entering through the doors. Then, if he moved quickly, he could exit should that be necessary. Wasserman leaned his head against the window and took a deep breath.

Finally there is time for a little rest, he thought.

The doors snapped shut. Forty-five minutes, less than

an hour, he told himself, before he'd arrive at his stop. Then just a five-minute walk and he would be home.

"The end of another day—almost," he muttered with quiet resignation.

The car's dull, yellowish light flickered as the train pulled away. Wasserman relaxed in its dimness, sufficient to see but not glaring like a spotlight. He could disappear and be anonymous, safe. It was as though his body had evolved over the course of his long, difficult life to blend into the background. Wasserman was short and frail, almost cadaverous, with grayish skin that seemed to change hue with the surroundings. No matter the commotion around Wasserman, his face remained placid. His thinning gray hair was always neatly combed straight back in a style typical of men his age. He always wore faded white shirts and brown pants that hung loosely, making him seem shapeless. His countenance suggested: "Keep your distance. I'm not interested in getting involved." His overall appearance was so ordinary and his manner so unassuming that strangers who came face-to-face with him could rarely describe him from memory.

Each day Wasserman rode the train into the city. Over the years he had perfected a strategy to avoid conversation with other passengers. He would sit without moving and kept his eyes fixed on the floor, careful to avoid meeting the gazes of his fellow passengers. If someone asked him a question or spoke a kind word, Wasserman would feign deafness, staring straight ahead, not moving a muscle. If the passenger persisted, Wasserman would softly hum a

Yiddish melody recalled from his childhood, a melody that brought him pleasant memories of Warsaw, Poland, when he was a young boy.

When in the city, Wasserman trudged from store to store gazing in windows, passing the time. Not because he was interested in buying but because the activity was free and did not attract any undue attention. And the time passed quickly and unceremoniously. By six o'clock, Wasserman would realize he was hungry and walk to Wolfman's Cafeteria, his favorite, where the air was redolent with the aroma of garlic, onions, and strong coffee. Each day he ate the same meal: stewed prunes, potato kugel, a warm bowl of borscht with a large dollop of sour cream, and a piece of thick black bread. The hustle and bustle—the clank of dishes, the hum of animated Yiddish conversations—created the perfect atmosphere for Wasserman to blend in and disappear. After eating he would take his glass of hot tea with milk and sugar along with a cheese strudel. Wasserman sat sipping his tea and nibbling his strudel until eight o'clock, the hour he departed to catch his train home.

But lately Wasserman had grown weary of his routine. He was often preoccupied with the past and had difficulty concentrating on the moment. The slightest distraction would cause his mind to wander. Images of his early life in Poland haunted him. To make matters worse, lately he was awake much of the night, tossing and turning, reliving vivid scenes of Auschwitz.

Wasserman leaned his head back and placed his hands between his bony knees for warmth. The hum of the train wrapped around him like a soft blanket, and he closed his eyes but fought the urge to sleep. As the train gained speed and the rocking became more pronounced, Wasserman felt his body relax, and his eyes slowly closed. The steady hum of the train grew fainter and fainter. And in spite of his efforts, sleep came suddenly and snatched him away to distant places.

Wasserman was jolted awake by the sudden scream of brakes. His old bones rattled as he jumped. When he opened his eyes, Wasserman was confused. He rubbed the sleep from his eyes with the back of his hands as the train rolled to a stop. When the train door opened Wasserman was enveloped by a gush of cold air that tightened like a vise around him. He saw movements at the door, and a man, woman, and boy appeared.

The man, who looked to be in his late twenties, was short and stocky. His puffy, unshaven cheeks jiggled as he walked. His head was covered with dark stubble. Two swastikas, one on each side, were tattooed on his muscular neck. He wore a pair of faded jeans held in place by a thick black belt and, in spite of the cold, a black, short-sleeved T-shirt. His black leather vest was decorated with SS lightning bolts, two on each side, and a skull and crossbones emblem on the back. The word s-k-i-n was tattooed in black ink on the four knuckles of his left hand, and a spider web was etched on his right forearm. The young man's chapped lips were twisted into a scowl. In the dim light, his watery eyes appeared yellowish.

Wasserman wanted to flee but because the young boy took so long boarding, his path of escape was blocked by mother and son.

Trapped, Wasserman cursed his misfortune. Why not in this life just a little mazel?

He quickly looked away just as the three approached the bench directly across from him. The footsteps of the young man and woman rang out like the heavy boots of marching soldiers. The boy's steps were muffled and reminded Wasserman of the shuffling of a prisoner being led to his fate. Drawn to these sounds, Wasserman, partially blinded in his left eye by a cataract, carefully shifted to steal a peek at the boy. He saw a boy, about seven or eight, his hair cropped close, almost shaved, giving him an older look. His angular, pale face had a pushed-in nose and was expressionless. The boy's fleshy ears, beet red from the cold, were set too low and protruded like fins. His left arm was bent and curled against his chest as though he were clutching a treasure. The boy's legs were twisted, making it difficult for him to walk and keep his balance. As the boy struggled to the seat across from him, Wasserman noticed the youngster's filthy, ill-fitting army boots; the right one worn at the toe from the constant dragging. Wasserman thought he could see the boy's dirty sock through the worn spot. He had seen others with this affliction but rarely as severe as the boy's. Wasserman felt a stab of compassion but quickly told himself that it was the boy's problem; he had his own tsuris to contend with, after all.

As the three settled on the bench directly across from

him, Wasserman instinctively, nervously covered his left forearm with his frail right hand hiding with another layer the six faded numbers tattooed on his wrinkled skin.

Of all the things, Wasserman bitterly complained to himself, an empty car and they decide to sit so close. Like a magnet I am for these types.

He watched the young woman steady her son, as he was having difficulty taking his seat without losing his balance. It was unusual for Wasserman to watch anyone so indiscreetly, but her gentleness and her son's complete confidence in her were seductive. Wasserman learned in Auschwitz as a boy of twelve not to stare and to blend in whenever possible. It was how he survived the camps—made himself invisible to the club-carrying *Kapos*.

As the train pulled from the station, Wasserman told himself to ignore the three and make himself as inconspicuous as possible. Maybe then the trip would end without incident. Sitting motionless and staring at the floor, Wasserman's thoughts traveled back to Auschwitz, the eighth day of January, 1944, Saturday, the Sabbath. It was the twelve-year-old Wasserman's first morning during roll call, and a guard, one who was liberally dispensing punches and kicks, was methodically progressing down the line asking children their ages. Wasserman saw the guard hesitate for a brief moment, then write in his notebook when a boy gave his age as thirteen. The boy, short and stout, was the type to survive, Wasserman thought. However, Wasserman also saw the bemused look on the guard's face as he wrote. It was a look that served as a warning to Wasserman. When Wasserman's turn came to give his age, he answered immediately in a strong voice, looking past the guard, "Fifteen."

Wasserman waited.

The officer paused and studied Wasserman for a few moments and then mumbled something in German that sounded like an insult but took no notes and moved to the next in line. Wasserman turned his head and stared at the boy, wondering if he had noticed that the guard had taken his number. But the boy was oblivious to the clues around him. Wasserman instinctively understood at that instant their fate was determined, and his knees almost buckled because of his gnawing fear, not knowing whether he made the right decision.

Wasserman soon learned he had.

Later that morning, Wasserman saw the boy marching with a group of women and young children to a low, single-story dirty brick building with unusually small, opaque windows. Towering over the roof were two, smoke-stained chimneys that continuously emitted a light gray, almost vaporous smoke that was carried beyond the camp by the relentless wind. Wasserman never again saw the boy. It was on that cold Sabbath morning in January that Wasserman realized that to survive Auschwitz he would have to blend in and watch for clues, be more cunning that the rest. This lesson he never forgot.

Wasserman heard a commotion across the aisle, and he saw the young boy had knocked over a bag of groceries his mother had placed in the seat next to him. Cans rolled everywhere.

"Why are you just sitting doing nothing?" the young woman chided her husband as she frantically collected the cans. "Can't you help with Zach or with anything?" Then after a short pause she began, in a voice simmering with anger, "If you . . ." but caught herself, knowing where the line was drawn.

"You're the one who wanted to bring Zach—we could have left him at your old man's place. So you deal with it, Sarah," the young man retorted defiantly.

Wasserman shrank further into his seat. Anxiety gripped his stomach.

Oy, just what I need to see—a family fight, Wasserman thought as he quickly looked away. In the silence he heard a series of noises: the crinkling of a cellophane wrapper, the tearing of paper, then the striking of a match. Wasserman heard the young man inhale greedily, and almost immediately Wasserman smelled cigarette smoke. The smoke irritated Wasserman's nose, and he suppressed the urge to sneeze. Evidently Wasserman unknowingly grimaced because the young man became angry and taunted, "You don't like cigarettes, old man? They're not your thing? You've got a problem with me smoking?"

Wasserman froze and continued looking down at the floor, motionless.

"Jason, leave the old man alone. He's done nothing to you," the young woman scolded in a low, careful voice.

Wasserman cringed inside but didn't move a muscle.

Then he glanced furtively at the woman and thought he saw her smile weakly, almost apologetically at him. He listened for any hint of what was to come next. But nothing happened. Thank God for the woman, Wasserman thought, maybe the rest of my ride will be peaceful, his usual gloom replaced with cautious optimism.

As the train approached the next station Wasserman hoped the three would exit. But they just sat and bickered through the stop. In spite of his efforts to ignore the three of them, there was something about the woman that drew Wasserman's attention. Her looks were striking; she was smallish, tiny actually, with a delicate, perfectly balanced face. At first glance Wasserman thought she looked insignificant next to the bulk of her husband. But her eyes, dark pools of sorrow, told a complex story and drew him in.

This woman has plenty of secrets. Such a story she could tell, Wasserman thought.

Her dark hair, curly and abundant, seemed alive and cascaded down to the middle of her back. The young woman wore tight black jeans and a black leather jacket that accentuated her lean body. Like her husband, she too displayed tattoos. Matching swastikas adorned the tops of each hand; the ink was fresh and retained a deep blue color that seemed to glow against the canvas of her olive skin.

Wasserman observed how all the young woman's attention, every bit of her interest, was directed to her son. She was protective and tended to his every need with remarkable tenderness and skill—wiped his mouth of excess saliva, put her arm around him so he could maintain balance as he sat.

Wasserman noted that the young woman deftly avoided her husband by tending to her son whenever he said anything to her or the boy. Her apparent stoicism regarding her son's pitiable condition and the casual way she ignored her husband's insults convinced Wasserman the woman had a backbone, was of high quality. But what caught Wasserman's eye most, what made him almost straighten in his seat, was the young woman's face. She looked Jewish; hers was a face from the shtetl. It was unmistakable—her hair, the shape of her face, her dark eyes and olive complexion. This girl, Sarah, was a Jew; well, maybe not now, but she had Jewish roots. Wasserman was sure of it. It is possible, Wasserman tried to convince himself. In one generation everything can be lost for a Jew in America. First the language goes. Besides Wolfman's Cafeteria, where could he hear Yiddish anymore? Then customs disappear. Even at his shul it was getting almost impossible to make a minyan for the morning prayers. Often one of the men had to search the streets for any unsuspecting Jew and drag him in to have the necessary ten Jews for prayer. And it wouldn't be long before the rabbi would jump ship to a wealthy congregation in the suburbs, and the synagogue, on the verge of bankruptcy, would be boarded up.

It is possible she is a Jew. In this country where half of the Jews live like goyim, anything is possible, Wasserman lamented.

Wasserman once again looked at the young woman, and just for an instant their eyes met. Wasserman offered a tentative, cautious smile, and he was sure he saw a brief, conspiratorial tilt of her lips in return, a smile that seemed at once to brighten and soften her eyes.

Suddenly the young boy rose from his seat and began moving across the aisle towards Wasserman, but before he could take more than a step his father grabbed him by the arm and slapped him hard on the thigh and yelled, "Sit down! How many times do I have to tell you!"

Wasserman grimaced, and his heart skipped a beat.

The boy choked and began to sob.

"See what you've done? You've hurt Zach," accused the young woman, her narrow chin quivering. "All he was doing was standing and stretching. You know he can't sit for a long time," she cried as she adjusted the boy's clothes and wrapped her arms around him. Distraught, the young woman felt the back of the boy's pants and yelled, "See what you've done now. He's had an accident. If you would act like a normal human being these things wouldn't happen."

"Me, it's my fault? What did I do? The kid's useless, a weakling. He better toughen up. That's why everybody picks on him. He's got to toughen up, that's all," the man argued in a voice charged with anger and frustration.

Suddenly, he jumped up from his seat and snapped impatiently, "Come on, here's our stop, let's get out of here."

As the train lumbered into the station, the young woman's eyes met Wasserman's again, just for an instant. Wasserman thought she looked desperate, like she was searching his face for a signal, anything to convince herself he was someone she could trust, confide in. He was sure the woman wanted his help. But before Wasserman could look away, he realized the man had seen him peering at his wife.

Without the slightest forewarning or provocation, the young man raised his arm and crudely aimed his index finger at Wasserman as if it were a revolver and spat, "Bang, bang, old man." Snickering, he continued, "You can run, old man, but you can never hide. Remember that, you can't hide." The young man looked even more menacing than he had when he first stepped into the train. Fear and revulsion paralyzed Wasserman. Instinctively, his breathing slowed, and his eyes remained fixed, looking into the distance, unblinking. He sat motionless, trying to become invisible.

Dear God, what does this one want from me? Wasserman thought. Don't move, God, don't move a muscle, he screamed at himself. Don't let the meshuga know I saw him. I've survived worse. This crisis will pass. I know it will, it always does.

After several moments, the young man lost interest in Wasserman and yelled at his wife and son, "Sarah, I said let's go, it's late. I want to get home," and stomped out the car. Wasserman felt a wave of relief as he exited.

The young woman said nothing but nervously nestled the boy into her arms and drew him close. She struggled with her son and shuffled her feet to regain her balance under his weight.

Wasserman watched her intently. He felt a growing connection, a bond with her. If she would just look at me before she leaves, then I could reassure her, he cried to himself. He felt sorry for her and wondered, How could a Jewish girl get involved in such things as this? He was certain she was different from the rest. Though he felt an urge to look away and blend into the background and hide, a wave of desperation swept through him, and Wasserman felt an overwhelming desire to reach over to her and touch the back of her hand. Instead, he stared at the young woman and edged forward in his seat and began to muster the courage to say that he could provide sanctuary, a room for her to escape from her husband. All she needed to do was stay in the car and let the doors close. Then she and her son would be safe.

But suddenly, without warning, the young woman spun around and found Wasserman staring. Their eyes met, each measuring the other trying to make sense of what was happening. Wasserman was certain he saw a smile in her eyes. Her warmth penetrated Wasserman, and he felt himself surrendering to her.

If I just talked to her and explained that things don't have to be this way she would accept my help, my friendship, he thought. Wasserman chided himself for his cowardice, urged himself to approach the young woman, but just looking, maintaining eye contact, took all his strength.

Because Wasserman was mesmerized, lost in his thoughts, he didn't notice that the young woman's eyes had turned cold and dangerous and narrowed like a predator's. Her soft neck was now taut, muscles and veins visible, her prettiness covered by a mask. Her face no longer reflected Jewish Warsaw, but goyish New York. The young woman, her lips blood-red lines, said in a practiced voice, a voice razor sharp with hate, "What are you looking at, you old, miserable Jew? Why don't you mind your own business?"

Stunned, Wasserman felt the air gush out of his body, and he slumped in his seat. He continued to stare at her without moving, afraid that if he moved the young woman would continue her assault. In the fixed silence of the car, the woman's words reverberated. He felt naked, exposed. Wasserman's face flushed with shame.

After a few moments the young woman abruptly turned away, dismissing Wasserman with a shake of her head, like an adult tiring of a pesky child. She turned and kissed her son on his forehead and said to the boy in a wistful, protective voice, "Zach, don't worry about Daddy. He won't hurt you. Everything will be all right. I promise you, everything will be all right."

From just outside the car on the platform, the young father threatened ominously, "Come on, let's get out of here. Everything takes so damn long with the two of you. If you can't deal with Zach, I will, goddamit. I'm telling you, I will get him moving."

The young mother's face twisted with dread. She moved quickly towards the door, almost tripping in her haste, holding her son tightly to her body, covering him like a shield. As the young woman held her son, the boy's jacket and shirt lifted, exposing the top edge of his grimy diaper and an ugly discoloration on his ribs. A gift from the boy's father, Wasserman thought matter-of-factly.

The door finally closed, separating them—the young

woman on the platform and Wasserman still motionless in his seat, sweating profusely.

Wasserman watched her struggling with her son, trying to keep up with her husband. The boy, attempting to walk quickly, lurched forward with an awkward gait. His mother was frantic, helping him along, pushing, trying to save him from a beating. When the three of them finally reached the exit, the young father whirled around and grabbed his son by the jacket and dragged him up the stairs. Wasserman saw the boy's face contort in terror. Wasserman turned away from the painful scene and saw his own expressionless face reflected in the glass. His deep set eyes were like those he saw in his dreams. He looked out again, but the family had disappeared into the night. The train suddenly lurched. The only evidence that they had been in the car was a slight hint of fruity perfume mixed with the foul odor of a dirty diaper and a balled up, empty pack of Camels the young man had thrown on the floor. Wasserman fought a wave of nausea and tried to swallow the rising bile. The bitter taste was overpowering. Sitting motionless, Wasserman took several slow, deep breaths trying to regain his composure.

"They're gone, thank God. Maybe now I can relax. Why let these anti-Semites ruin my ride?" he muttered.

But rocking to and fro in the moving car, Wasserman could not relax because he knew that even though he was fortunate today, this same scene would play again, if not tomorrow, then the day after tomorrow, and the next time he might not be so lucky. He also understood the inevitability of what lay ahead for the young woman and her son and said in a voice barely audible, "No, my little shiksa, no, it won't. Things will not be all right."

The train lurched around a curve, causing Wasserman to momentarily lose his balance. "So much I have seen on trains—enough for two lifetimes," he sighed, more with resignation than sadness. He felt strangely at peace in the moving car, as if the train was headed back to Warsaw, Poland, to happier times, to a time before Auschwitz. Even the bitter taste began to dissipate. He felt the protective shell encase his body, his equilibrium slowly returning. The steady hum of the train soothed like a lullaby beckoning Wasserman to sleep, but he fought the urge to doze and thought, nightmares now I don't need. Instead he listened to the silence, the language he understood. Wasserman looked out the window and saw bright, twinkling lights shimmering against the vast dark sky. At first glance the lights of the city seemed cheerful, even promising, but he knew it was an illusion because just beneath the sparkle lay the deception; to be safe, a Jew had to understand that things might not always be what they seem. He thought about the young mother and how she had deceived him. I mustn't be such a fool and be tricked so easily by a young pretty face, he scolded himself. I can't be so careless as that. He smiled weakly as he looked around the dimly lit car and was grateful he survived his stupid mistake. The little shiksa was right, he thought. I should mind my own business.

Wasserman pushed back in his seat and leaned his head heavily against the window and drew a deep breath. He was overcome with a sense of calm. Finally, a little peace and quiet, at least till the next stop, he thought to himself. The solitude pleased him, momentarily. Then the clanking of the train brought to him memories of his transport to Auschwitz a lifetime ago. Images of Jews squeezed into boxcars, like herring in a barrel—the pushing, the shoving, the kicking, the screaming. The six numbers on his left forearm burned red-hot, testy companions for over sixty years, reminders to always be wary. I must listen to my instincts more carefully next time, he warned himself again. In a well-practiced manner, he crossed his legs, hooking his right foot behind his left ankle, and hugged himself tightly so he took up as little space as possible. Then, thinking about the several stops yet to endure before he would exit, Ira Wasserman wearily closed his eyes and curled his shoulders, making himself smaller, less visible for the rest of his lonely ride.

Kaddish for Two

"It's the Abramovitch curse!" Zev Abramovitch wailed as he lurched out of his chair towards his son, who was sitting stiffly on the old Naugahyde sofa.

"Dad, what has a curse got to do with anything? All I said was I don't have a girlfriend." Scooting to the edge of the sofa, he continued, "Anyway, can we change the subject; there's something I need to talk to you and Mom about."

Ignoring him, Zev, his black eyes burning like hot coals behind thick, tortoise shell glasses, barked, "Look at you! You're a grown man. Men get married and have families. You should have children by now, Aharon. It's the first commandment in the Torah—be fruitful and multiply! And let me ask you this, Mr. Big Shot—at this rate, without a son, who will say kaddish for you? . . . No, let me finish. Too many in our family haven't had sons to say kaddish for them. And now it's happening to you. It's a curse, I tell you, it's the Abramovitch curse!"

Hearing Zev screaming yet again about the family curse, Fanny bolted from the kitchen with speed and agility that belied her age and size. Zev and Aharon turned at the cracking sound of the two swinging doors hitting the wall as Fanny bounded out of her kitchen. With her, a waft of freshly baked apple-cinnamon strudel filled the living room. As she wiped her hands with the towel she always carried, Fanny moved her ample frame between her son and her husband of forty years. Aharon smiled to himself as his father shrank before this force of nature. Her mere presence seemed to cast a spell over Zev. As his wife approached, Zev cast his eyes downward as if he were already embarrassed for the dreadful scene that lay ahead.

"Not the curse talk again, Zev. God in Heaven, what kind of man quotes from the Torah, 'be fruitful and multiply,' to his son? Of all the passages you choose. With so many boys making babies outside marriage! Such a brilliant husband I am fortunate to have," Fanny said, readying for more sparring.

Zev, knowing he was now treading in dangerous waters, shuffled two steps back, then tried to defend himself, but Fanny, her gray hair spilling loose from the bun on the back of her head, was unwilling to listen.

"Zev, leave Aharon alone! You're always so fast with the advice. It's always the needle with you. Forty years I have to listen to the curse talk. This aggravation continues, and you will be saying kaddish for me," Fanny said.

"The boy needs to find someone, get married, have a family," Zev piped, puffing out his chest. Then, sighing with regret, he continued, "The system was better in the old country. Fathers decided who their children married.

Aharon would have had a bride on my timeline," Zev said, beating his chest with his right hand. "We'd be grandparents already. The sons by now he would have!"

"Don't get started with the good-old-days business again, Zev," Fanny retorted, her hands planted firmly on her hips. "Nothing was better in Russia. You don't remember why our families left? Conscription in the Czar's army, that's what you think was better? So many Jewish boys taken from their homes and forced to serve twenty-five years in the army. Remember Yitzok and the khapers?"

"What are khapers?" asked Aharon.

"Kidnappers. They stole boys for the army, sometimes taking youngsters only eight or nine years old," Fanny groaned. "No child was safe. Oy, God, I will never forget it when Yitzok was snatched. He was only ten. And the poor parents, Zev! Like zombies they were from the grief. The way Russians treated Jews, that's what I call a curse!"

Aharon began to relax and watch the drama unfold. He was familiar with these lengthy and sometimes philosophical skirmishes. Zev and Fanny continued, ignoring Aharon. He wondered, with all their constant bickering, what kept his parents together. He sometimes tried to imagine them young, carefree, in love—he couldn't. Their marriage was a great mystery to him.

"Aharon is thirty-two years old and still a single man, Fanny. Thirty-two already and no prospects," Zev complained.

Shaking his head in disbelief, Aharon interrupted,

"Dad, you lost a year. I'm thirty-three and, believe it or not, happy and not looking for marriage prospects."

"Oy, gevalt, may God help us," Fanny moaned, "thirty-three years old and still not married! Aharon, listen to your father. He has a point—you're not getting any younger. Goldie Hemelfarb, you know, my friend who lives on Fifth Avenue, she has a beautiful daughter, Marsha. She's single! You remember her. You saw her at Kupperman's wedding, a couple of years ago. The sturdy one, built just like her mother. The disposition of an angel, she has. And smart! She is even a secretary for a fancy lawyer downtown. The money that girl must make! It should happen to you, Aharon. I can call Goldie and set up . . . "

"Marsha Hemelfarb!" Zev bellowed. "Disposition like the angel of death, she has! To this day I have not seen the girl smile, not once. With her it's constantly the pinched face. Aharon, don't listen to your mother. Nothing but tsuris that girl will bring you."

"I can't believe this. Our conversations go nowhere. I can see why, from day one, I never had a chance," Aharon groaned, burying his face in his hands.

Zev marched to the back of the living room and planted himself in front of the family tree. Zev rarely missed an opportunity to talk about the Abramovitch family.

"Enough talk of that Hemelfarb girl. That subject is kaput, finished. Fanny, come sit here, close. Aharon come too, you must hear what I am going to say."

Aharon listened to his father's voice—such a confident, enthusiastic voice. He felt his opportunity slipping away.

"Dad, there's something important we need to talk about. Can we talk now?"

"You have something more important than the curse? This you're not interested in?" he asked, looking chagrined and motioning towards the family tree. "For your information, Mr. Not Interested, you are descended from a family of great distinction, just remember that. Now let me finish. Then, if you want, we will talk."

Resigned to their fate, Fanny and Aharon trudged to the two chairs facing the family tree. Aharon and Fanny knew Zev's stories well; he had told them many times over the years. Aharon let out a loud sigh and thought, there must not be a compassionate God. He would not make me sit through this.

Zev positioned himself just to the left of the family tree and stood behind the small table where he stored records of the Abramovitch family history. Aharon watched his father prepare. It occurred to him that this little area of his parents' house resembled the bema in their synagogue, and his father's lectures, which often included biblical references, were sermons.

Aharon, preoccupied, nervously pulled at his closely cropped beard, anticipating how his parents would react to his news. He thought, Why now, why tell them today? Maybe I should wait for a better time? But he knew there would never be a good time to break this kind of news. It might as well be today. At least tonight they will have Sabbath dinner to calm them down, he reassured himself.

Biding his time, Aharon studied the Abramovitch

family tree. Oh, how his father loved the family tree! It was a work of art, he had to admit. The family tree covered much of the wall. Each name was typed and perfectly spaced. A small photograph or, if one didn't exist, a sketch painstakingly created by Zev based on family lore, appeared over each name. Each branch trailed to distant lands. There was the Russian branch reaching back to the time of Napoleon's invasion of Russia. Zev told of relatives from all walks of life—artisans, merchants, money lenders, pious Talmudic scholars, and poor, suffering Jews who were persecuted and murdered in pogroms. He told of the family's great Talmudic scholar, Avrom, and his wife Gittle, who lived their entire lives in Minsk. Another branch found its way to Poland, to the rein of Casimir the Great, known as "the King who was good to the Jews." A third branch led to Budapest, Hungary, back to the eighteenth century, to the time of Joseph II, when the Abramovitch women played significant roles in the family history. Zev always spoke proudly of these women who were pious, with practical, razor-sharp minds, and ran households and family businesses, working day and night to allow their husbands to study in the beit midrash. And there were others, cut from a different cloth; his father spoke in awe of the raven-haired beauty Renee, who, as a young girl, ran away and joined a traveling acting troupe and performed in Yiddish theaters throughout Hungary. "The great Sarah Bernhardt, huh? A nothing compared to our Renee, I'm telling you, a nothing," Zev boasted. And so the stories would go on . . .

Aharon saw his father's yarmulke, prayer shawl, and prayer book lying on the table. He remembered being a child, how the gold designs on his father's prayer shawl and skull cap glittered in the light and drew him to his father like a warm smile, how he would sit close and listen to his father's stories. Seeing the objects now, however, he thought of another incident: when his father, much younger and thinner then, tried to teach Aharon, age ten, to put on phylacteries. "Your grandfather, your namesake, taught me; now I must teach you," he said. "Look here, Aharon, first you wrap the strap around your left arm . . ." Aharon still remembered his own words because it was the first time he stood up to his father, his first of many rebellions: "I'm not going to do it, put those things on . . . I don't care what you do." A line drawn in the sand. Aharon never forgot the argument that followed, the lingering disappointment of his father, or how his mother, running from her kitchen, came to his rescue, demanding that Zev "be a mensch" and leave Aharon alone. As he made his escape that day, Aharon realized the power his mother held over his father.

"Aharon," Zev challenged, "are you listening to what I'm saying? With you it's always the daydreams. The Abramovitch curse is a black cloud and has wreaked havoc on our family. So many of us have not had sons to say kaddish. And now maybe the curse, God forbid, has struck you."

"Zev," Fanny screamed, "again, the curse talk. Like a dog I've suffered hearing about the curse for so many years . . ."

"We have all suffered from the Abramovitch curse,

Fanny." Zev pointed to the family tree with one hand while he adjusted his glasses with the other. "Aharon, look at Yankel, Avrom and Gittlel's only son. He spent his whole life at home, studying the Talmud. My grandfather, may he rest in peace, told me Yankel had the keenest of minds. He wrote scholarly commentaries that were studied throughout Russia. Another Rashi that boy was! But he never married," Zev said, jabbing his finger toward a face on the wall. "He had no wife, no family, no son. Legend has it he had to pay someone to say kaddish for him. Can you imagine such a thing? A stranger, not a son, saying kaddish. Think of it, Aharon, no son to say kaddish or light the yahrzeit. No son to remember you, to carry on your name. You will never rest in peace. What kind of circumstance is that for a Jew? What kind of parents are we to allow such a goyish thing to happen? Oy, you don't know the worry this has caused me . . ."

"Of course the man didn't have a wife or son. He was the shtot-meshugener," Fanny interrupted.

"What's that?" Aharon asked.

"The town fool," answered Fanny. "A keen mind! The man probably didn't have enough sense to come in from the rain. Huh. He was a schnorrer, Zev. He probably spent all his time sitting in the market waiting for handouts. How could he have a wife and family, Zev? That's what you call a curse? Bad luck, maybe, curse, no!"

"Always with the kibbitzing, Fanny. Can't you let me finish when I am talking to my son, just for once? Oy, the headache I'm getting from all the interruptions."

Sighing deeply and rubbing his forehead, Zev began again. "Aharon, it has been passed down that the Abramovitch curse began with your great-great-grandfather, Meyer. His only son Mendel did something, something shameful, against Jewish law. Family legend has it Meyer and his family were driven from Minsk by the beit din, the rabbinical court. They just vanished, dropped off the face of the earth. Mendel must have been influenced by Satan himself for the rabbi to excommunicate him and curse the family. And to this day, Aharon, the curse stands. That's why so many Abramovitch men have not had sons to say kaddish, I'm sure of it!"

"Zev, that was generations ago. What kind of man dwells on the past?" argued Fanny.

"The past you say," Zev said, pointing a stubby, callused finger at a photo of a man with sharp features and round, furtive eyes. "Well, what about my cousin Sidney from Chicago? Remember when he came for your bar mitzvah, Aharon? I can't tell you the money that man made during the war. Rich like a king, and a tzaddik, too, that's cousin Sidney."

"Draft dodger," Fanny yelped, "Sidney was a draft dodger—that's how Sidney and the rest of them made their money, buying and selling scrap metal when all the other men were fighting the war. A real hero our Sidney is. The finagling that when on was shameful."

"Scandalous, talk like that is scandalous, Fanny," Zev screamed. "Don't be a gossipmonger. The man had a verifiable medical condition that kept him out of the war. Such a thing to say about an Abramovitch, and to your own son, no less. Such an example to set, Fanny."

Zev turned impatiently to the family tree and groaned, "Aharon, now you see what I have to put up with, forty years of interruptions. Your mother is always getting me off track. No wonder my stomach constantly has the gas. What I am trying to say, in spite of their money, the Abramovitch curse struck them too. There is no escaping the curse. Look here at Irving, Sidney's son—a good-looking man, a real mensch, but he's fifty years old and not married. Sidney told me Irving never had a girlfriend. The worry this has caused your uncle Sidney you'll never know. The tsuris that poor man has suffered. Who can say why such a thing happens? Another Abramovitch who will not have a son to say kaddish once he's passed on. This is just one more example of what I'm talking about, Aharon. It's the Abramovitch curse, I tell you!"

"Ach, Zev, Irving has a nose like a ram's horn, that's why he never married," Fanny countered, pointing frantically to the picture. "Look at him, his head is shaped like the map of Israel. The curse is Sidney was too cheap to pay for a nose job for his son. We can thank God our Aharon has my family's nose, the Goldstein's straight nose."

"Stop with the noses talk, Fanny . . . "

As Zev and Fanny continued bickering Aharon looked at the family tree. He studied the faces of Yankel and Irving. Something about them caught his attention. He leaned forward and fixed his gaze first on one, then the other. Fear shadowed their faces. Their eyes were furtive, yet sad. Aharon had seen that look before. He felt a jolt of recognition, a sudden realization that Sidney and Yankel shared something with him after all. Is this the Abramovitch curse, the reason so many of us don't have children? he asked himself. This is the black cloud hanging over our family? Knowing it was time to finally reveal his secret, Aharon took a deep breath and said, "Dad, Mom, could you both please just listen to me? I have something important to tell you."

Zev and Fanny stopped talking and, startled by the interruption and the urgency in Aharon's voice, peered expectantly at him.

"It's not going to happen—I'm not going to marry Marsha Hemelfarb or anyone else. I have been waiting a long time to tell both of you," Aharon said, wrapping his arms around himself. "Oh, how do I say this," he groaned. "I am . . . I have been for as long as I can remember . . . I'm . . . I'm gay," Aharon stammered. "That's why you have never seen me with girlfriends. That's why I won't have a son to say kaddish for me. Dad, it's not the Abramovitch curse. I'm gay."

Zev and Fanny sat speechless, dumbfounded, and exchanged glances. Zev shook his head, as though he hadn't quite heard his son. His fingers closed and opened mechanically as he grabbed the arms of his chair, trying to keep his balance as he sat. His face turned ashen, but his eyes darkened and narrowed to slits. "What is this you're telling me and your mother?" Zev asked, weighing each word carefully.

"Dad, I'm gay. I'm sorry it took me so long to tell you and Mom, but please try to understand. It doesn't change anything. It really doesn't. I still love you both. I . . . I'm just gay, that's all."

"That's all? That is what you say? Fanny, your son says it won't change anything," Zev said. "That's what you think, Aharon, nothing will change? Everything for your mother and me will be the same, that's what you're saying? Your mother can talk to her friends about her son, how he likes to spend his time, lead his life? And what do I tell my friends when they ask about you, Aharon? And what about the little matter of finding a nice Jewish girl and having a family? So nothing changes, that's what you think?" Zev cried, his voice choked with anger.

Confused, Fanny interrupted, "Gay . . . what is this gay? . . . I don't understand." Then, turning to Zev, she pleaded, "What is this gay business, Zev?"

"Fanny, our son is telling us he likes boys. He sleeps only with boys. Girls . . . for reasons only God knows, girls he doesn't like." He said these words angrily and with contempt.

More perplexed than ever, Fanny stammered, "Doesn't like girls? What's not to like about girls?" Fanny looked at Zev and Aharon and asked softly, "How is it possible to . . . to sleep . . . oy, how is such a thing possible? Somebody tell me. I can't in my mind picture it."

Zev, his face beet red, his lips stretched thin, quivering with rage, exploded, "Don't try to picture it Fanny; you don't want to imagine such a thing. How can you do this to us, Aharon! How can a good son do this, bring dishonor and shame to his parents? It's an abomination, I tell you. Everything we have done for you—the schools . . . money . . . opportunities, everything. A father and mother never loved a son like me and your mother loved you. And this is our return, our repayment? This is how you say thank you? This is what a good Jew does? If you cared anything about us, you'd change, make things different. My whole life, your mother's whole life—a sacrifice for you. And you decide to do this to us?"

"But, Dad. . . ." Aharon interrupted, but before he could finish, Zev, his face contorted with anger, leapt to his feet and barreled out of the room. Shoving the kitchen door open, he stomped to the back door, slammed it closed, and left Aharon and Fanny sitting in stunned silence.

Aharon and Fanny stared at each other, frozen in their seats. Fanny winced as the swinging doors creaked to a stop. Her eyes were red and watery. Finally, she placed her hand on Aharon's shoulder and squeezed gently. "Aharon, just try, can't you listen to your father, just this once?" Then she added softly, "I'm not sure your father can accept this. As a Jew, he's suffered many things, but this, Aharon . . . I just don't know. You have no idea how much your father loves you, worries whether you will be all right. Your father, I know him, will think it is his fault you are . . . you know . . . ."

"You can say it Mom. Gay. It's not a bad word," he said sharply. Then, checking his anger, continued, "Mom, you don't understand. It's nobody's fault. It's just the way it is. If I wanted to I couldn't change. I'm gay, and I like being gay. That's who I am. I have been for my whole life, ever since I can remember. Mom, I'm sorry, but it's not going to change."

Aharon shifted in his seat and, moving closer to his mother, asked in a strained voice, "Mom, can't you talk to Dad, make him understand and accept this? Please, I know you can help, Mom. You always know what to say to him. He will listen to you. He always does."

Fanny shook her head and sighed. "Oy, such a world we live in. In Minsk I never heard such strange things. Sometimes there was the evil eye or dybbukim, but never such a thing as this—this gay business . . . "

"Mom, please talk to Dad, he'll listen to you . . ."

"Aharon, what do I say to a man like your father? He has suffered such things you'll never know. And now this. He would never tell you about the insults growing up, indignities at work, always the outsider. Everyday, outside the house, you don't think your father sensed their distaste for him, just because he was a Jew? How does a man adjust to such a situation? I'll tell you how. Everything is black and white to your father, either right or wrong. This way of thinking makes life easier for him because choices are clear. In forty years, not once have I seen him change his mind, never!"

Taking a deep breath and slowly shaking her head back and forth, Fanny, with a look of resignation, continued, "What can you do if God wants it that way? This gay business—what you are doing is wrong to him. There is no other way he can see it. Aharon, how can you expect to reason with a man like that?"

Fanny and Aharon looked at each other and sat silently. Finally, Fanny sighed and added, "Aharon, there was a saying in Minsk when I was a girl, 'If your wife is short, bend down and listen.' Aharon, short I am, but whether your father will bend and listen to reason, that I can't tell you. I just don't know. Promises I can't give."

Shifting in her seat and looking at Aharon, Fanny said in a quiet, guarded voice, "I'll need some time alone with your father. I'll talk to him tonight, over a big meal. Yes, that's it. I'll make something special. That's the best way, a stuffed cabbage and a nice kugel for dessert. That will calm his nerves. Come to the house tomorrow morning after your father has gone to services. Maybe by then he will accept this—this gay business . . ."

Aharon escaped from the room, his head pounding as his racing thoughts collided, and he heard his mother mumble to herself, "Oy, such a thing. How can a boy, such a nice, good-looking boy, not like girls?"

Bounding up the steps to his parent's home the next morning, Aharon noticed that the blinds were closed and the curtains were tightly drawn. "That's odd for ten o'clock in the morning," he murmured. The image of the shuttered house put him on edge. The house that held so many memories for him now seemed changed, somehow transformed into something unfamiliar. Standing on the front steps, Aharon hesitated, afraid of what he might find.

Taking a deep breath, he pulled the door and it opened with a harsh squeak, like an alarm. He was startled by the eerie darkness inside. Standing motionless, he noticed the absence of the familiar smell— no rich aroma of a freshly baked strudel—no warm, comforting heat from the oven. Instead, the air was cold and damp, the house dark and hostile. Stepping into the foyer, Aharon looked up and was shocked to see the mirror covered by a bath towel. He stared at the covered mirror with growing unease. Aharon's heart pounded. No, he thought incredulously, Dad wouldn't go that far. He wouldn't.

"Mom, it's me, Aharon," he called tentatively, peering into the darkened living room. But there was no answer. From his parents' bedroom at the back of the house, through the closed door he heard the soft, muffled weeping of his mother.

Aharon crept toward the bedroom. The anxiety in the pit of his stomach worsened with each step. He passed the family tree. The entire Abramovitch clan watched him through the grayness. Scanning the room, he noticed a lone, flickering candle casting a faint yellow glow on his father's prayer book, which was opened to the kaddish. In the dim light, the book looked menacing.

Aharon cautiously opened the door to the bedroom, and he glimpsed his mother sitting on a footstool near her bed, barefoot, in the dark. Wrapped around her, completely covering her upper body, was her prayer shawl. Holding it tightly closed, Fanny rocked back and forth as though she were moving to the internal beat of an ancient rhythm.

Shocked, Aharon gaped at his mother for several moments, unwilling to believe what he was seeing.

Fanny looked up and cried, "I tried to talk to him, to explain. I pleaded. Did everything I could. But it was no use. All night we argued." Her sobs came in rapid order as she gasped for breath. "I never saw him so hurt, so angry. In forty years I never saw your father like this, like demons were in his head making him say such things. He said we do not have a son, that we must sit shivah . . ."

Aharon stood frozen, listening. The walls of the room wobbled before his eyes, and he felt dizzy, nauseated. He tried to compose himself, to say something, anything, to comfort his mother, himself, but the words weren't there. He just stood and stared at his mother as she continued to cry, her sobs coming in short bursts. Except for Fanny's bitter weeping the room was filled with a cold, angry silence.

He yelled in a rush of despair, "No! Damn it, no," then fled from the room and ran out the front door with the image of his grieving mother accompanying him as he raced down the street toward his father's synagogue, struggling against the raw, swirling wind.

Shaken, breathless Aharon jerked open the synagogue door and saw ten old men, their threadbare overcoats and mufflers thrown over the backs of the pews. The men, all refugees from Russia like his father, were bent over their prayer books.

Seated on long wooden benches, the men looked like old, neglected gravestones crumbling in an ancient shtetl cemetery. Books, their Hebrew letters like carefully arranged fragments of skeletons, were everywhere—on benches, on tables that lined the sides of the synagogue, stacked into a pillar on the bema.

Aharon imagined the old men as lookouts, preparing for an attack. Flanking one side was Mr. Glatstein, frail, bent like a question mark, his enormous white beard dwarfing a bony face, his lips moving fervently in silent prayer. Across the aisle sat several others, also hunched over their prayer books but whispering in animated conversation, their Yiddish words evaporating in the thick air. All of it reminded Aharon of many colorful tales his father told of life in Minsk—the yeshivas and their young scholars; thriving, overcrowed markets; the ranting of the Hasidim; arranged marriages turned sour. A time long forgotten and abandoned, except for these remnants who gathered on Saturday mornings.

Then he noticed his father sitting in his usual seat, on the far side, completely alone, an old, defeated Jew who had withdrawn into himself.

Aharon hurried up the aisle, feeling a pain he had never experienced before, and sat directly behind his father. Pairs of suspicious eyes turned all at once to study the intruder, examining his every move. He felt like a specimen under a microscope. Aharon inhaled deeply, attempting to steady his breathing and put in order his confusing thoughts. "This can't be happening!" he mumbled to himself, over and over.

Zev sat with his head bowed, oblivious to Aharon

sitting just behind him. He appeared to Aharon smaller, diminished, like the immigrant he was, with his fractured speech and shattered dreams—exiled, yet again. At the bema, the rabbi and cantor stood slowly, the weight of the world on their narrow, stooped shoulders. The rabbi commanded all mourners to stand for the kaddish. Aharon sat and watched as his father slowly and with difficultly rose to his feet, clutching his prayer book with trembling hands. Stains from the tears of many others were visible on the pages. With his powerful body bent forward and his feet spread, it looked as though he were bracing himself against a storm. In a chorus of men, Zev, his voice sounding like a wail, began the ancient chant . . .

"Magnified and sanctified be the great name of God. . ."

Aharon winced as he heard the first line of the kaddish, as if each word were a punch from a fist. Magnified and sanctified, magnified and sanctified, he repeated over and over. Just words, he thought, words that mean nothing, a torrent of words. Looking over his father's shoulder, Aharon's eyes were drawn to the rabbi and cantor—bookends, both ancient with immense white beards, each wrapped in a tallit, looking as though they belonged to another era, cohorts with his father in a conspiracy against him. After all the years with Dad and Mom, Aharon thought, the Sabbath dinners, the family talks, the walks to the synagogue, the endless fights, all the prayers chanted together, the tears shed, after all that, after everything we've been through, to not know, to not understand each other, seemed impossible.

Aharon closed his eyes, and faces of the Abramovitch family passed before him, one after another, filing into the synagogue, as though summoned by his father to join the minyan. Aharon listened to his father chanting the prayer. From his father's lips, each word of the kaddish cut through the air, slicing into him. He wanted to scream at the top of his voice, "Dad stop, please stop! Why are you doing this to me?" But instead he stared at the faded gold etchings on his father's tallit and now understood them as fool's gold, nothing more. He felt the gulf between him and his father widen. He wanted to stop the steady progression of the prayer but was powerless against its ancient rhythm. And so, with the persistence of a marching army, the chanting of the kaddish quickened.

"May God's name be blessed and praised and glorified . . ."

The sound of rain hitting the synagogue windows filled the sanctuary. A dirty light seeped in, blanketing everything, hovering in the open spaces between the benches, blurring the distinct shapes of the men. It looked to Aharon as if the mourners, rocking to the cadence of the kaddish, were praying in a fog. The damp air sunk into him and made him shiver, and he wondered if it was a sign from God— a branch of the Abramovitch family would now whither away and not bare fruit.

Each line of the kaddish added weight to his burden. The room closed around him; he felt confined, pressed for air, as though he were encased in a coffin. Aharon felt emptiness in the pit of his stomach, and in this void, anger grew. You narrow-minded son-of-a-bitch, he thought bitterly. Two can play at this game. Aharon stood defiantly, and for several moments he simply glared at his father and listened to the words of the prayer. Then Aharon joined the chanting, at first tentatively, then more forcefully as though he were hurling words at his father. Together, Zev and Aharon, their sad, angry eyes fixed on the page before them, spat out the prayer for the dead . . .

"May God grant abundant peace and life to us . . ."

With silky, black kippah in place and prayer shawls draped over their shoulders, Zev and Aharon appeared almost identical. Their strained voices were in perfect harmony as they continued chanting the kaddish. It was as though the old world of Minsk had finally assimilated into the new: continuity, a passing of the torch. And Aharon tried to understand—had the Abramovitch curse struck again and brought him and his father to this turning point, a breech, a separation of their paths, or was the curse simply one generation failing to understand the dreams of the other? Standing just behind his father, Aharon saw his emotion, a pink flush creeping slowly from his cheeks to his ears, visible through his gray stubble. Zev wrapped himself tightly in his tallit, as though he were comforting himself for the long, lonely journey ahead. In a surge of anger, Aharon considered grabbing his father's tallit by the fringes and ripping off the protective covering, exposing his father to the pain he was inflicting. So it was a mystery to him why, chanting the final lines of the kaddish, he felt closer to his father than ever before. Aharon's knees buckled as he was overcome with a crushing fatigue, and he fought with all his strength to remain standing. In spite of his exhaustion, Aharon felt a powerful urge to reach out and hug his father and not let go, to whisper in his ear, "Dad, I love you." But then his heart hardened, and his neck stiffened, and he thought better of it. Instead, Aharon closed his eyes, raised his angry fist to the heavens, and cried the final words of the kaddish . . .

". . . and let us say: Amen."

Leonard Saperstein & Company

~~~~~~

"Leonard Saperstein and Company, how may I help you?" answered Ida Nudelman. "I'm sorry to tell you, Mr. Flexner, Mr. Saperstein passed away three days ago. He is no longer with us," she said, her voice choked with emotion. After a deep breath she continued, "Yes, it was a shock to all of us. A cerebral hemorrhage, in his sleep; thank God he didn't suffer. The doctor told us—I mean, informed the family—Mr. Saperstein died instantly. How old? He would have celebrated his seventy-fifth birthday in just a week. No, he didn't, Mr. Flexner, he didn't look his age—such energy and vitality. And what that man overcame in his life. He was such an inspiration to all of us! We still can't believe it. Mr. Saperstein founded the company fifty years ago. No sir, Mr. Flexner, Arthur isn't here. He is sitting shivah with the family. We don't expect to see him until Monday . . ."

Ida Nudleman, Leonard Saperstein's personal secretary for some forty-five years, hung up the phone. Impeccably dressed in a dark blue winter suit and a white silk blouse with matching pearl earrings and necklace, Miss Nudelman, in her early sixties, wore her thick graying hair in a tight bun held in place with a silver clasp. Navy blue pumps accentuated her still shapely calves. Ida, through moist, watchful eyes, looked across the room at Hannah, a small, skittish, dark-haired woman, who sat at an ornate, mahogany desk just a few feet away. The young woman, completing her first week as staff secretary, had been listening intently to the phone conversation. Before Ida could return to reminiscing about her years working with Leonard Saperstein, Hannah inquired solicitously, in a tremulous voice, "Miss Nudelman, are you all right? Can I get you anything?" Ida Nudelman's mascara had begun to run, staining her cheeks with dark blotches.

"It's still such a shock, such a blow," Ida said, looking into a compact mirror while dabbing her eyes with a lace handkerchief she'd taken from under the sleeve of her left arm. "I still can't believe he's gone. Mr. Saperstein hired me forty-five years ago when I was your age, Hannah, just twenty years old. He gave me an opportunity," she said, choking back more tears. Then, after sighing deeply, added breathily, "And if I say so myself I took full advantage of my opportunity."

"Really? How so Miss Nudelman?" Hannah asked, shifting her gaze from Ida's dark, penetrating eyes to her perfectly manicured hands.

"Oh, yes, I took full advantage. Mr. Saperstein hired me as general secretary—in fact, the very same position you occupy. But I had set my sights higher; I wanted to be Mr. Saperstein's personal secretary. Mrs. Krasner occupied that position when I started here. But when I met Mrs. Krasner . . . well, first impressions tell you everything about a person, Hannah. Just looking at her I knew she wasn't the right woman for the job. She wasn't at all fashionable. She was too drab for an office like this. You will come to understand, Hannah—a good administrative secretary sets the tone; she is the heartbeat of an office."

Hannah straightened the wrinkles in her own dress and wished she had worn her more stylish blue one instead.

"She was too dumpy. Her figure suggested indulgence, lack of discipline, no commitment to her responsibilities— not stellar characteristics for someone in an important position. Don't you agree, Hannah?" Ida asked, her sculpted eyebrows raised.

"It sounds like she was just a mess," said Hannah, holding in her stomach and sitting straighter.

"And that wasn't the half of it! I saw that our Mrs. Krasner didn't execute the little details a man like Mr. Saperstein expects."

"What happened? How did you get promoted?" asked Hannah, thoroughly engrossed in the story.

"I took advantage of Mrs. Krasner's complacency. She was under the mistaken impression the job would always be hers. But she was in for a rude awakening. I studied, learned quickly, and soon made myself indispensable to Mr. Saperstein. That's the trick, to make yourself indispensable. You must do all the little things that allow them to concentrate on important matters. If Mr. Saperstein needed a file, I made sure it was on his desk immediately, before he asked for it. If he took clients to dinner, I chose the restaurants and made the reservations. I can't tell you, Hannah, the hours I spent studying menus so I could pick restaurants that were just right for the occasion. I learned what each client liked to eat and drink so I could select the place that was perfect for Mr. Saperstein and his guests. You've got to talk to clients, develop a personal relationship so they're comfortable revealing themselves—their likes and dislikes. Take Mr. Orenstein, for example. In time, Hannah, you'll get to know him. He's a compulsive little man, a finicky eater, but he's one of the richest, most successful men in the city. And you know what he told me years ago, when I first met him? He'd traveled from one continent to another, seen fantastic wonders, and eaten in some of the most expensive restaurants in the world, but he would trade all of that for just one more plate of his mother's tzimmes. Can you imagine that, Hannah? It's the mother-son bond that is so important, particularly for Jewish men. Mr. Orenstein was not only looking for a plate of hot tzimmes, but a warm heart. Well, soon after I began work here, Mr. Saperstein scheduled a dinner meeting with Mr. Orenstein to try and convince him to give us his business. It was a potentially lucrative account—very important to us at the time. So I went to work, did some research, and found out his mother had emigrated from Białystok, Poland, in the early 1900s. Jews from Białystok were famous for their tzimmes. So I found an old Jewish cookbook and discovered original recipes straight from the shtetl."

"What made their tzimmes so special?" Hannah asked.

"The women prepared a special potato kugel topping and combined prunes and apricots, not one or the other; in Białystok, it was both. Then I called Katz's deli and asked if they would prepare a special order for Mr. Saperstein. Well, when Mr. Saperstein and Mr. Ornstein arrived, Mr. Saperstein told him he had already ordered and had a surprise. Mr. Saperstein told me that during the meal Mr. Ornstein kept crying out, 'Oy vey, Leonard, such a gift you have given me! It's just like mama's tzimmes. And the dumpling, ah, such a dumpling!' Mr. Saperstein told me Mr. Ornstein would have agreed to anything that night! That's how an administrative secretary does her business, Hannah. It's all in the details. They've got to trust you, your judgment, Hannah. You build that trust from the first day. They soon understand, almost instinctively, that you know best in these matters. That's how you climb to the top, Hannah. Always anticipate their needs and do more than you're asked. Within six months I was promoted and became Mr. Saperstein's personal secretary, and I have been ever since," Ida said proudly, momentarily forgetting her grief and returning her handkerchief under her sleeve in one swift motion.

"What ever happened to Mrs. Krasner?" Hannah asked.

"Mrs. Krasner . . . how shall I put it?" Ida leaned forward, her eyes narrowed. "Let's just say Mrs. Krasner saw the handwriting on the wall. But it really doesn't matter. My point, Hannah—she wasn't right for Mr. Saperstein, and it was better for everyone, including her. Mrs. Krasner knew it was time—you always do when your time is up. You can feel it—the tension in the office, the lack of support. It's not what anyone tells you, Hannah, it's what they *don't* say. Suddenly you are treated with less respect. You are made insignificant. At first they don't ask you to do little things, the things you have always done. Then you're out of the loop when decisions are made. Your opinions are not deemed important or helpful. At some point everyone must face this, the changing of the guard. Life moves on, Hannah. It stops for no one."

Hannah turned, grabbed the sweater that hung on the back of her chair, and draped it over her shoulders. "Brrrr, it's chilly in here all of sudden."

"That's how Mr. Saperstein liked it. He said it was best for keeping everyone alert, attending to their responsibilities. Mr. Saperstein used to say, 'No one daydreams in a cold office.' I set the thermostat at sixty-eight and make sure no one touches it."

Ida looked over to the thermostat, her body instinctively poised, ready to pounce, if necessary. "Forty-five years it's been sixty-eight degrees in this office, and sixty-eight it will remain!" Shifting slightly in her seat, Ida continued, "Poor Mr. Saperstein used to complain his wife kept their house too warm. He said it made him sluggish, drained of creative energy."

"Miss Nudelman, tell me about Mr. Saperstein's wife. It seems odd to me there are no pictures of her in his office."

"Mrs. Sap . . . oh, I shouldn't say this, but," Ida leaned forward and carefully parsed her next words, "theirs wasn't a happy union. They had too many differences. Mrs. Saperstein wasn't sophisticated enough for a man like Mr. Saperstein. I really think, and I hate to be so blunt, particularly under the circumstances, but Mrs. Saperstein was an embarrassment to Mr. Saperstein."

"Really, in what respect?" Hannah asked, her dark eyes wide and riveted on Ida, hanging on her every word.

"Oh, don't get me wrong, Mrs. Saperstein has many wonderful qualities. But like everything in life, relationships are complicated, and those of a man and a woman . . . well, even the great psychologists are unlucky in their attempts to completely understand them, Hannah. They both emigrated from Serokolia, a tiny village near Łódź, Poland. If I am not mistaken, they were about ten years old when they came to America. Apparently Mr. Saperstein's father was some important rabbi over there, but after they arrived, the only job he could find was doing piecework in a sweatshop. He barely eked out a living, even though he worked from dawn to dark. That's how it was, Hannah. Mr. Saperstein said his father told stories of renting a sewing machine each day from one boss to work in the shop of another. It was a terrible setback for their family. But in America, what good was a rabbi who couldn't speak English, no matter how many books he wrote in Poland? Mrs. Saperstein's family was no better off. Her father, too, was a religious Jew; he was a cantor, but who would listen to the voice if the songs were from the shtetl? Like many who came to America to find their dream, instead they found a nightmare. In America, Hannah, the streets weren't paved with gold, at least for many in that generation of immigrants. Mrs. Saperstein's father finally found work at a delicatessen—from chanting to chopping. Life, Hannah, has its hard edges. But, in spite of these difficulties, the two families remained close through the years. My theory is, and it is only a theory: the Sapersteins had an arranged marriage. I'm sure of it. You're too young to know, but that was common back then. Religious families arranged marriages to ensure their children would maintain observant homes.

"Unfortunately, this match wasn't made in heaven. Over the years Mr. Saperstein studied, learned, and worked hard, rose above his beginnings; he assimilated. Mrs. Saperstein didn't, like lots of Jewish women then. Even now, after all these years, she speaks with a Yiddish accent. Mr. Saperstein spoke beautiful English, not the slightest trace of an accent. You would never guess he came from Poland. And another thing, Mrs. Saperstein is almost Orthodox—keeps a kosher home, observes all the holidays, the whole nine yards. She couldn't break from Jewish traditions."

Ida leaned forward and waved her finger at Hannah, emphasizing her words. "It was a terrible strain on Mr. Saperstein running a business under such difficult circumstances. Most Fridays Mr. Saperstein and I worked late, until eight or nine o'clock, so he often missed the family's Sabbath dinner. That was a constant source of conflict between them. I can't tell you the phone calls that poor man suffered through. 'No work on the Sabbath!'

she'd scream. And you know how deeply a woman's tongue can slice. Mrs. Saperstein never assimilated, never understood the business world, the pressure on a man like her husband. What's that expression, Hannah, 'you can take the girl out of the country, but you can't take the country out of the girl'? Let's just say Mr. Saperstein was Hart Shaffner Marx, and Mrs. Saperstein is the sale rack at Kline's," said Ida, smiling at her own cleverness and displaying perfectly straight, white teeth. "The poor thing has no sense of style. She was not capable of traveling in the same circles with Mr. Saperstein. Don't misunderstand, Hannah, tradition is important," she said, unconsciously stroking the diamond studded Star of David that hung at her neck. "But Jews have to change with the times; they have to blend in."

At that moment, the two women heard a noise at the door, and in stumbled Arthur Saperstein. Rumpled from the wind, his dark, wavy hair was blown in every direction. His wrinkled blue shirt was only partially tucked. His navy sport jacket, hanging loosely and at least two sizes too large, was wrinkled and didn't match his slacks. Arthur's chunky body and unshaven, jowly cheeks made him appear more like a clerk in a bakery, one who'd nibbled too many rugelach, than a business executive. The expression on his round face was pensive and pouty, as though his heavy gait required excessive concentration and effort.

"Arthur . . . Mr. Saperstein," Ida stammered, "What in heaven's name are you doing here? Why aren't you home with your family?"

"Hi, Ida," Arthur said as he absentmindedly brushed his hair from his forehead and walked slowly across the room.

"We have a houseful, so I thought I'd sneak over here to get a few things done. With all the activity at the house, no one will miss me. Believe me, mother is well taken care of."

"We were just talking about your wonderful mother," Ida said, shaking her head. "How is Mrs. Saperstein? Is she holding up, the poor dear?"

As she said this, Ida cautiously rose from her seat and stared at Hannah with narrow, penetrating eyes.

"Mother is doing surprisingly well, Ida. Having all her friends visit with her has been a great comfort. Fortunately, mother has a wealth of friends."

"Thank God for that," Ida said. "Can I get you coffee, Mr. Saperstein?"

"No, thank you, Ida, I'm fine for now. There's enough food and drink at home to feed an army."

Then he turned and looked over at Hannah who had stood up at her desk. "Hello, Hannah. Are you getting settled into your new job?"

"Oh, yes, Mr. Saperstein, I've had a wonderful week!" Then, moving towards Arthur, she quickly added, "But I want to tell you how sorry I am—"

Before she could finish, Ida nimbly maneuvered between Arthur and Hannah and said, "Excuse me, Hannah, but Mr. Saperstein, as he said, has work to do. I'm sorry Arthur, I will make sure you are not disturbed with idle chitchat."

Annoyed at Ida's interruption, Arthur began to say he

rather enjoyed talking to Hannah but instead turned and walked across the reception area.

Ida raised her eyebrows slightly as he thumped past his own office and entered his father's.

Darting toward him, Ida called in a tentative voice, "Arthur, is there anything I can help you find?"

Arthur didn't answer, began to close the office door, then stopped, looked past Ida and said, "Hannah, call maintenance and have them bring ten packing boxes for me and my swivel chair from my office, will you, please?"

Before Hannah could answer, Ida, throwing her arms out, interrupted, "But Mr. Saperstein, I will go downstairs myself and bring . ."

"Oh, no, thank you, Ida, I prefer Hannah to call."

Before Ida could say another word, he closed the door, and Hannah was on the phone, leaving Ida looking uncomfortably out of place.

After Hannah hung up the phone, Ida, her face twisted into a scowl, turned to her and hissed, "Like a peasant he dresses. It's no wonder the man can't find a wife—thirty-five years old and no family. It's hard to believe Arthur is Mr. Saperstein's son."

"What do you mean, exactly?" asked Hannah, still excited about being asked to make the phone call.

"Oh, everything I suppose. Now don't get me wrong, I've nothing against Arthur, may God grant him a long and healthy life, but they're just so different. The man doesn't have his father's, how shall I say it, his drive, energy, his decisiveness." Ida leaned towards Hannah and whispered,

"I shouldn't tell you this, but Mr. Saperstein joked more than once that he sometimes wondered if Arthur was a hospital mix-up."

Looking briefly at Leonard Saperstein's office, she began once again, choosing her words carefully. "Arthur is truly his mother's son. It's such a shame, Hannah. Mr. Saperstein was a tzaddik, a blessing from heaven, there is no other way to put it. I just don't know what's going to happen to the company now that Mr. Saperstein is gone. Even Mr. Saperstein had doubts that Arthur has what it takes to manage the business. I know I shouldn't say that, but it's God's truth!"

"Oh, how awful and sad. Didn't Mr. Saperstein ever have faith in his own son?" asked Hannah, a pained expression twisting her youthful face.

"Oh no, it wasn't always that way, Hannah. You have no idea the plans Mr. Saperstein had for Arthur. Even at Arthur's bris, and I remember it like it was yesterday, at the end of the ceremony Mr. Saperstein lifted Arthur high into the air for everyone to see and said he finally found a business partner! This made an impression on me, Hannah, because it's written that what a boy sees and hears at his bris, he becomes. And for the first few years it looked like Mr. Saperstein had indeed found his business partner. Arthur was the jewel in Mr. Saperstein's crown. Those were the happy days. But like all good things in this life, Hannah, it didn't last."

Ida shifted in her seat, leaned toward Hannah, and continued, "To understand, Hannah, you have to know a little Saperstein family history. It was soon after the bris, not more than a year or so, that Mr. Saperstein got sick. I remember it was in the summer, after Mr. Saperstein and his family returned from vacationing at Grossinger's. The illness came so suddenly. Mr. Saperstein first complained about a few aches and pains; then fever came. We thought it was a bad case of the flu. But a week or so later the polio struck full force and changed everything."

"Oh my God! What a dreadful thing to happen," Hannah cried, transfixed by the story.

"It was tragic," Ida went on. "A new father struck down just like that. But Mr. Saperstein was one of the lucky ones. Only his legs were affected. Even so, he was out of the office for months, first in the hospital and then at home getting therapy and regaining his strength. In his absence, I took over, Hannah, even though my parents tried to persuade me to quit and find another position. They were afraid I'd contract polio from Mr. Saperstein. I can't tell you the fear in those years. No one understood how you contracted polio. But the thought of leaving Mr. Saperstein never even crossed my mind, Hannah, never!"

"I can't imagine what it would be like living with something like that," Hannah said, pursing her lips and wrapping her arms around herself.

"It is a sign of strength, Hannah, when a man overcomes adversity, and Mr. Saperstein did just that—overcame. But there is always a cost to pay when you are faced with such a challenge."

"Cost . . . ?" asked Hannah, looking perplexed.

"Of course, Hannah. The polio changed Mr. Saperstein. At first the change was small, almost imperceptible. I noticed he was more impatient with himself—angry he couldn't do many of the things he did before. As time went by, Mr. Saperstein became more demanding of everyone, especially Arthur. And I saw Mr. Saperstein's disappointment in Arthur grow over the years. Arthur didn't excel in school, didn't have the drive of his father. Mr. Saperstein always pushed him to accomplish more. When he finally graduated from college, Mr. Saperstein wanted him to join the business immediately, but Arthur, with his mother's encouragement, I might add, squandered an entire year. Can you imagine such a thing? And when Arthur finally began working here, well, it didn't pan out the way Mr. Saperstein imagined it would. I can't tell you the terrible arguing that went on between Arthur and his father. It was always about the same thing: Arthur did not live up to his father's expectations. You have to understand, Hannah. Arthur has never shown any interest in the business. His attitude always seemed . . . spiteful."

"But—" Hannah began.

Interrupting, Ida quickly added, "Oh, I know Mr. Saperstein could be a difficult and demanding father, but I don't think that is an excuse for Arthur's ungrateful attitude toward his father. Do you, Hannah?"

"I can't comment about that, Miss Nudelman, but in the short time I've worked here I haven't seen them argue, not one time," Hannah countered. "Arthur seems the perfect son, a gentleman."

"Well, the last few years have been better, fewer arguments, but only because Mr. Saperstein stopped giving Arthur any real responsibility."

Ida shifted slightly in her seat and, with a grave look on her face, continued in a whisper, "It's a great tragedy for everyone, Hannah, when a son disappoints his father . . ."

Out of breath from packing boxes, Arthur walked to his father's enormous oak desk, plopped in the padded swivel chair, and ran his hands over the smooth desktop and the ornately carved edges. The feel of the smooth surface sent a shiver of excitement through him. He marveled at the sturdiness of the desk, his father's prized possession.

The large office was sparsely but elegantly furnished and carefully arranged so Leonard Saperstein could easily maneuver in his wheelchair. There were two matching armchairs with silky, blue and gold trimmed seat covers on either side of the desk. An Italian black leather couch was positioned in the middle of the room facing the desk, with enough space for Leonard to wheel to the couch and talk to his visitors. The heavily polished oak floors gleamed and made a fast track; there were no carpets to impede the movement of Leonard's wheel chair.

On the walls hung several expensive paintings, abstracts in bold colors, done by famous Jewish artists whose names Arthur could never remember. There were also photographs depicting important events in Leonard Saperstein's professional life—Leonard shaking hands with the governor and accepting various civic awards. In all the photographs, the straight, hard lines of Leonard's face reflected not the pleasure of accomplishment but the fatigue of a battle hard-fought.

Arthur leaned back in his chair, opened his newspaper to the obituary page, and looked at several death announcements written by his father's admirers. One caught his eye: "Saperstein, Leonard—A man of integrity, strong character, and noble spirit. A mensch and Yiddishist who never forgot his poor beginnings in Serokolia, Poland. Devoted husband and father who gave his time, talents, and money to the March of Dimes. We, his friends and colleagues, extend our deepest sympathies to his loving wife, Bess, a woman of estimable character and elegance, and to his son, Arthur. May his memory be a blessing . . ."

Arthur put the paper down and considered what might be written in his own obituary, but nothing in particular came to him, and he quickly dismissed the thought. He looked down at the newspaper again and read the words "strong character, noble spirit." Try living with that strong character and noble spirit, he thought to himself, rubbing the stubble on his fleshy chin. What had his mother once, in a fit of anger, called his father? "Street angel and house devil." May his memory be a blessing, indeed.

Arthur opened the top middle drawer of the desk and saw his father's custom-made appointment book. The cover was scuffed, almost grubby from a year's worth of use. It was stuffed haphazardly with loose notes, newspaper clippings, and letters. Arthur read several of the letters, all business related, and a few of the notes written by Ida in her careful hand, reminding his father of meetings, dinner engagements, birthdays, and travel plans. Arthur was struck by Ida's devotion to his father and how she had painstakingly organized everything for him. The central role Ida had played in his father's life and how little room he had left for his mother was never more evident to Arthur. A twinge of resentment grabbed him.

It was then that an old photograph buried among the papers caught his eye, a photograph he'd never seen before.

Arthur picked it up and peered at it—a picture of his family when he was a baby, one of the few photographs he had seen of his father before he got sick. Why would his father keep this photograph at the office? he wondered. He angled the photograph so the light better illuminated it. His father, holding the infant Arthur in his arms, impeccably dressed in a suit and tie, standing well over six feet tall, towers over his mother. He appears strong and healthy, his broad shoulders tapering to a narrow waist and long, straight legs. His mother is wearing an ill-fitting housedress and seems out of place next to his father's elegance. His father, with a confident and optimistic smile, looks generations removed from Serokolia, while his mother's feet seem firmly planted in the rich soil of the shtetl.

Arthur studied his father's face and lean, athletic body, radiating energy across space and time to find a sign, any look of weakness or distress or fatigue in his father's eyes, but there was no hint of the illness that was soon to strike. Nor was there a glimmer of his father's unpredictable, explosive anger. His open, optimistic face appeared incapable of twisting into a mask of vitriol. Arthur wondered whether the seed of his father's anger had always been there, an artifact carried over from Poland, or had it been born out of the pain and disappointment of his illness? Growing impatient with himself, Arthur thought, What good comes from speculating about things in the past? He got sick, and that's that.

Arthur returned the photograph to the appointment book and flipped through the pages, studying the notes his father had written. As he read, his father's dominant voice leapt off the pages. After reading for several minutes, he turned to his father's last notation, written just a few days earlier in strong, perfectly formed letters. "Have Ida prepare Steinmetz materials for Monday phone call to Jake Steinmetz." Then, directly underneath, his father had added, "I have a hunch Irving is turning the business over to Jake. Need to move on this."

Arthur stared at the page for several moments and shifted in his seat. Why hadn't his father told him about the Steinmetz change? He tightened with anger. The book was a written record of how little his father confided in him on important matters, a record of a father's low regard for his son. Arthur snapped the appointment book shut and held it for several minutes. Then, taking careful aim, Arthur tossed it across the room into the wastebasket. "Perfect shot," he said, smiling thinly, surprised by his accuracy.

As Arthur returned to the work of packing up his father's belongings, he thought of something that had happened just a few weeks earlier. Late one afternoon,

Arthur, thinking his father had left for the day, walked into his office to retrieve a file. Arthur was surprised to find his father still there, sitting not in his wheelchair but on the couch, his legs extending almost its full length. The only light came from the windows across the way, giving the room a diffuse, eerie glow. Before Arthur could apologize for barging in, he saw that his father was grimacing as he rubbed his outstretched legs. Arthur stood frozen for several uncomfortable moments, staring at his father, feeling like an intruder. Then he walked to the couch and stood close.

Suddenly, without looking up, Leonard, his eyes puffy and face drawn, said in a flat voice, "It seems my whole life is this goddamn pain."

At that moment, Arthur looked at his father's creased face, a face drawn from years of struggle, and he wanted to place his hands on his father's shoulders and talk to him, just once, without the awkwardness that was always a wedge between them. But something held him in place, and he just stood with his hands at his sides. Both men remained silent while Leonard continued massaging. The outline of his thin, wasted legs, visible through his trousers, was a stark contrast to his powerful hands and arms.

Arthur, growing more ill at ease in the silence, finally asked if there was anything he could do, any way he could help.

With his head still bowed, Leonard brusquely answered, "You have two good legs, bring me my briefcase from under the desk."

Arthur stood motionless, his face burning, and said

nothing. He fixed his eyes on his father's face. The office seemed to grow darker. Even after years of experiencing his father's sudden, unexpected flashes of anger, they still left Arthur shaken, diminished. Once he regained his composure, Arthur brought his father the case, and, after standing self-consciously for a brief moment, he walked out of the office and quietly closed the door. It was only when Arthur was in his own office, a safe distance away, that he felt sheltered from his father's disappointment.

Sitting in the office now, all of that anger and disappointment trapped in the past, Arthur couldn't remember ever feeling so relieved and in command. Thoughts of how he would now take control of the business rushed through his mind. "Yes," he told himself, smiling confidently, "I'm in charge now!"

Ida Nudelman looked nervously at Mr. Saperstein's office and muttered, "He's been in there for over an hour. What in heaven's name could he be doing?"

She jumped from her seat and skirted to the door. Accustomed to just strolling in, Ida instinctively reached for the doorknob but then hesitated and knocked, tentatively. Almost a minute passed before Ida heard Arthur call, "Yes?"

Once inside, she was dismayed by the sight of Arthur sitting at Mr. Saperstein's desk and the disarray in the office.

"Please, Mr. Saperstein, let me help you."

"No, thank you, Ida. There's nothing I need you to do right now," Arthur said. "In fact, why don't you and Hannah call it a day? It's almost five o'clock, no sense staying. I'll take any calls and lock the office."

"But I can stay, for years I—"

Before Ida could explain that of course she would stay and close the office as she'd done for forty-five years, Arthur interrupted curtly, "That will not be necessary, Ida, not necessary at all."

They glared, each sizing up the other, and after several long, uncomfortable moments of silence, Ida looked down and said in a voice suddenly small and brittle, "Well, if you don't need me, I suppose it is unnecessary for me to stay—"

Arthur slipped past her and called, "Hannah, before you leave look in my office and bring me the Steinmetz file. And while you're at it, turn up the heat, will you please? My God, it's cold in here."

"Yes, sir, Mr. Saperstein! Right away, sir," cried Hannah, her voice charged with excitement.

"Just one other thing, Hannah, would you mind coming in a few minutes early on Monday, at around 7:30? I must prepare for an important call to Jake Steinmetz, and I'd like your help. I've been studying the account, and I have a hunch that Jake will soon be taking over for his father," he said, almost believing his deception.

"Of course, Mr. Saperstein! I won't be a minute late." As Hannah said this she was already planning where she would stop and pick up coffee and rolls for Mr. Saperstein on Monday morning.

Ida slumped in her chair, biting her lower lip, her

face dark and frowning while the two spoke around her as though she was of absolutely no consequence. She began to perspire. Events were spinning out of her control. While Hannah scurried around the office, Ida fidgeted and straightened her already meticulously organized desk with fast, anxious hands.

When it came time to leave, both women gathered their belongings, then walked to the door immersed in thought. Hesitating for just a moment, Hannah, giddy and blushing like a young bride standing under the wedding canopy, abruptly turned to Ida and addressed her in a bold voice, a voice Ida had not heard before, "Ida, don't rush in Monday morning. I'll see to it the office gets started smoothly," and out she flew, leaving Ida reeling and fuming with bitterness.

Sitting in the deserted office, a wave of excitement gripped Arthur. In all the years he'd worked with his father he had rarely spent time in the office alone. His father was the first to arrive in the mornings, rain or shine, and Arthur always left for home promptly at five o'clock while his father and Ida stayed late and finished the day's paperwork and phone calls.

Sitting with his arms folded, Arthur turned his swivel chair, lifted and stretched out his legs, placed both heels on the grand desk, and leaned back. The feel of his heels on his father's desk gave him a thrill of guilty pleasure, and he felt taller, leaner, in-charge. He closed his eyes, savoring the moment. He was amazed how a day that began on a depressing, sour note could turn around and show such promise of new and exciting opportunities.

Maybe now, he contemplated, I'll join the health club. Mulling it over and over, unaccustomed to making decisions, he finally concluded optimistically: Yes, why not? I could stand to lose a few pounds, tighten up the mid-section.

Pleased with his emerging take-charge attitude, he drew a deep breath, and his pudgy body relaxed and molded itself to the contours of the soft leather chair. Arthur sat motionless and peered at the partially packed cardboard boxes scattered throughout the office. He figured it would take another hour or two of work to clear everything out; then he could begin refurnishing.

With each passing moment Arthur felt more and more like he belonged behind his father's desk. And with his newly found confidence he began to feel an unfamiliar interest in the office. Before, when his father ran things, almost nothing about the business interested him or held his attention, but now every detail, no matter how small, took on special significance. The pale green walls of the office caught his eye and struck a discordant note. It was as though the walls had absorbed his father's stern gaze over the many years and now radiated his disapproval.

I'll call the decorators on Monday to paint; a nice shade of blue will do just fine, he planned.

He also decided that he would cover the wood floors with a thick, burgundy carpet. No need for hard, fast surfaces anymore. Oh yes, things would be different now that he was in charge, he thought to himself. He was a man who knows his time has finally come.

Arthur took a deep breath and exhaled slowly. A self-satisfied smile appeared on his lips as the ever-present anxiety loosened its grip.

As the afternoon turned into evening, a sudden and powerful wind rattled the office windows. Startled, Arthur walked quickly to the windows to be sure they were tightly secured, then sat back down at the desk. He knew his mother expected him home soon to say kaddish and have Sabbath dinner, but he had no intention of leaving, not just yet. His mother would have to understand that he ran the company now, and his work responsibilities came first. While contemplating these responsibilities, which he now faced alone, a bead of sweat formed and rolled like a tear across his furrowed brow. Feeling suddenly vulnerable and drained of energy, Arthur twisted in his seat as the silence tightened around him, squeezing out his new confidence.

The phone rang. Arthur froze, and for an instant he wished Hannah were there to take the call, to run interference. At that moment, it seemed he had never felt more alone or unsure of himself. In the failing light of the early evening Arthur leaned back in his chair, clasped his hands and placed them under his chin, and closed his eyes for several long moments. Into the emptiness, Arthur breathed a soft moan that sounded very much like a prayer.

The Last Jew in Krotoszyn

Ruta Singer, the last Jew in Krotoszyn, Poland, stepped around a weathered gravestone and bent slowly to pick up pieces of broken wine bottles, balled-up newspapers, and several apple cores. She placed the refuse into a stained canvas bag and grunted her disgust.

"Ach, those miserable bums. All they know is to spend their time guzzling spirits and littering a sacred place. Such persistent shenanigans can only be the evil machinations of dybbukim. They'll be the death of me yet. Twice already this week I had to chase those vagabonds out. But it's not easy business. They take great pride in taunting an old woman who can no longer move swiftly. And if it's not them, it's the goats with their insatiable appetites for the flowers I plant. Each day in this life the Almighty sees to it there is a new, nasty surprise. But how much more can an old woman suffer? The aches and pains, Magda. Just to bend down I have to ask permission from the Almighty himself. And the tsuris an old woman like me has to face . . . Ach, thirty years ago, I could have caught them, those no-goodniks, and given them their comeuppance, a swift kick in the tuchas. But now . . . ," she gazed across the cemetery, a wistful look in her eyes. "Thirty years, Magda, a lifetime I've spent tending this cemetery—keeping it neat, orderly. The way it should be. Out of respect."

Ruta Singer grimaced, showing her few remaining teeth, and placed her bony hands on the bench as she slowly guided herself down. She was a wisp of an old woman who retained the confidence of someone who had once moved gracefully. But arthritis had played its dirty trick and stolen her mobility so that she had to coax every movement from her creaky, bent body. "Ah, Magda when I was your age . . . enjoy the gift of youth now, my little one, because in time the Almighty will play his trick on you too. That you can be sure of."

"Who is this, Miss Singer? The lettering is almost gone," said Magda, touching the raised edges of the carvings on a gravestone, not paying attention to Ruta's words. "Why is a bird carved on it?"

Ruta rose with great effort from her seat and limped toward the young girl, who was kneeling in front of the small stone, studying the intricate carvings. Ah, to have once again that enthusiasm and energy. Then a sharp pain grabbed her knee.

"Oy, this miserable left knee of mine. It feels ten years older than the rest of me. Why does the Almighty insist on making a special case of me?" Ruta complained. Am I being punished for not fighting hard enough against all that has happened during my lifetime? Is it maybe the Almighty seeking his pound of flesh because I haven't been a good enough Jew? As Ruta approached, Magda shifted her attention and looked up expectantly at the old woman. Sensing the impatience of her youth, Ruta said, "Be patient with me, Magda. Lately my walk has become nothing more than a mere crawl. But why hurry? Who wants to arrive early to their funeral? Why provide merriment for your enemies? Besides, if the truth be known, at my rare age I have the right to move deliberately. Did you know one reason the renowned sages were so wise is they, too, were at the age where they did everything slowly, with great care. And I have reached such a point in my life. Deliberation, my little one, is the first step toward wisdom."

Ruta saw that Magda was too engrossed in studying the carvings on the marker to pay her any attention. "Ach, why do I use what little breath I have left talking to you about such matters? But why expect more from someone so young who doesn't understand what life is like for an old Jew living in Poland? When I was your age I didn't listen, either. It's the curse of youth."

Ruta bent down and looked closely at the worn marker. The sun's rays danced on the gray stone, highlighting the fissures on its surface. "So, I see you have been drawn to the work of Pesach the stonecutter. He was a magnificent artist. Someone with such talent for masonry had to be born with a chisel in his hand. The Almighty chose for him early his destiny. And what better calling for an artist? Magda, look at the simplicity and beauty of the letters. No extraneous curls, no frills—just precisely cut lines. It's as though each letter was chiseled by a higher power," she said.

She directed Magda's attention to the top of the stone.

"But see how the limestone is being worn away by the passage of time and how the bird has almost dissapeared? One day these markers will be wiped clean of their stories. Even the artistry of a great stonecutter, Magda, is no match for the will of the Almighty. How is it said in your bible? 'The Lord giveth and the Lord taketh away.' My fear, Magda," said Ruta, slowly straightening and returning to the bench, "my fear is: what happens after me? There are no Jews left in Krotoszyn to carry on this sacred work, to keep the memories alive, to tell what happened to the Jews during the war. When I pass on to the next world, who will tell these stories, tend the cemetery? Time will erase all of these memories, and this sacred place will become a playground for those bums."

"Miss Singer, don't say such things! You will care for the cemetery for many more years," said Magda with a force that belied her age.

"Ah, little one, no one lives in this world forever. Besides, I'm not afraid of going on to the next world. Life here is no picnic, particularly for an old Jew in Krotoszyn. But Magda, a good Jew never loses faith that given a nudge, the Almighty might be persuaded to intervene and make life better in this world."

"Who is buried here?" asked Magda, pointing at a gravestone.

"So, you have finally met little Rivka. The poor thing was summoned to the next world by the Almighty when she was just about your age, Magda."

"What happened to her?"

"What happened to Rivka happened to many Jews during the war. If the Germans or the Russians didn't get you, the Poles did. And the result was always the same. But enough of that. I wondered how long it would take before you and Rivka became acquainted," said Ruta, chuckling quietly.

"Acquainted?" asked Magda.

"Your look tells me you actually think you discovered this cemetery and Rivka's stone accidentally, without a small nudge from a higher power. Did the question not occur to you why a young girl like yourself was drawn to helping an old Jew tend a cemetery? Like all youngsters, you think things in this world occur by chance, that there is no higher power who, with a grand design for each, pulls ever so slightly on our strings."

"I don't know what you mean," said Magda. "I just saw you one day in the cemetery working by yourself and thought you needed help. That's why I come every day."

"Sit," Ruta said, chuckling quietly and patting the space beside her. "Sit down right here, little one. Let me explain to you a few things, things about the Almighty and Krotoszyn." Magda sat and scooted next to Ruta. She felt the old woman's bony hip poking against her thigh. Ruta sighed and crossed her legs, "Ach, where to begin?" From inside her shawl she drew a white handkerchief and dabbed at her watery eyes.

"Every evening, Magda, when I have finished my work, when all the streets are empty, long after you have gone home, I sit right here among old friends and enjoy the quiet. Here the memories of my people come back to me, how it was in Krotoszyn before the war. Before they were all murdered." Ruta turned and looked around furtively and then leaned close to Magda and whispered, "That's when it happens, when I see a portion of the next world. The cemetery comes alive with those long departed. It's true! Believe me. See right over there, just beyond the hill?" Magda shifted and saw a grassy hill with a gravestone sitting on top, rising toward the heavens. "It's there I often see Bertha the unlucky. Every night she sits by herself, lamenting her fate, just as she did in this world many years ago."

"Why do you call her unlucky?" asked Magda, her eyes wide.

"In this world, Magda, Jews have the worst type of luck, but Bertha was one of the unluckiest. Both her husbands left her: husband number one for America, and husband number two, well, who knows to where he fled. In my estimation, neither husband was worth much. But I mustn't be too judgmental. After all, show me a wife who can be objective where her husband is concerned. And added to her marital disasters, Eizik, her beloved son who she considered to be the reincarnation of Moses himself, ran off and married a Polish girl and disappeared from the face of this earth. And the unlucky Bertha continues searching for him in the next world."

Ruta adjusted in her seat, took a deep breath, and continued.

"And that's not the half of what goes on, Magda. Oh no, not the half of it! Yudel the porter appears every night, too. And the distance that man traveled in this world. I'm telling you, little one, if you added all the kilometers that poor man lugged his cart and put them in a straight line, he could have traveled to Lublin and back again. Now he looks just as he did in this world—a mountain of a man. And you've never seen such a worker! He is stronger than any mule, and just as obstinate."

Magda gasped.

"Why the surprise, Magda? You don't think there is a need for a porter in the next world? You doubt that sometimes, even there, there are loads that require the help of someone with a strong back?"

Speechless, Magda just sat and stared at her old friend. Ruta began again, her words tumbling out like she was sharing an intimate secret that had been kept for too long.

"I see others, too: Rabbi Glussman and the poor Sonia Zemel, for example. How that woman has suffered, you'll never know. Her son, even in the next world, is still a bachelor! And I mustn't forget Lida Arenfeld. The stories I could tell you about that woman. I see all of them, generations of Jews, just as I see you now, Magda. The Almighty has deemed it necessary that I see just a little portion of the next world. I have learned this world and the next are two sides of the same coin, separate dimensions that exist side by side with lives being led simultaneously. It just took a little nudge from the Almighty, and suddenly I saw everything." Ruta made a face, shook her head, and added, "And frankly, this kind of thing is not necessarily what an old woman wants to experience."

Magda shifted nervously in her seat.

"I can see by the look in your eyes that you have doubts about the veracity of my story," said Ruta gently.

Magda shook her head and began to say that of course she believed Ruta, but before she could, Ruta shushed her.

"No, no, little one, you don't have to explain yourself. I understand, am sympathetic. When the Almighty deemed it necessary for me to see the other world many years ago, I thought the same as you—that I was seeing things that did not exist, that these images were evidence of the weakening mind of an old, lonely woman, that I was only a few short steps from a complete collapse, a breakdown. But I saw them as clearly as I see you now. And if it is true that only imbeciles question what is right before their eyes, then shouldn't the wise believe what appears before them? Just because I see things no one else sees, must they be the conjuring of a crazy woman?"

Ruta moistened her lips, drew a short breath, and continued.

"How long has it been, Magda, that you have visited me here in the cemetery? Several months? Magda, maybe it is your destiny that the Almighty will one day allow you a peek into the next world so that you, too, will know the history of Krotoszyn and how things were before everything was destroyed. And who knows, Magda, because my time is short, and as topsy-turvy as things are in this world, maybe the Almighty will enlist your help to tend the cemetery after I pass on. Maybe the Almighty has chosen you to serve as keeper of the stories."

The two sat in silence for several minutes. A cold breeze swept across the cemetery. A flock of geese in perfect formation flew overhead. Ruta scooted closer to Magda, put her arm around her, and then reached into her coat pocket to retrieve the cemetery key. Gently taking Magda's hand, she said, "Here, I want you to take the key and open the cemetery tomorrow morning and begin working without me. I have other business, business all old women must complete once in their lives." Ruta placed the key into Magda's palm and closed her fingers tightly around her hand. "Can I count on you, little one? Can I count on you to come tomorrow and begin working in the cemetery?"

"But why would the Almighty want me to tend the cemetery and learn all the stories? I'm not Jewish."

"Little one, what choice does He have? With all the calamities in this world and the next, I don't think He has time to worry about something small like that. A prophet I'm not, but I think the Almighty is not so much a stickler; He must be practical in matters such as this. If it's going to take a Gentile to keep alive the stories of Jews who once lived in Krotoszyn, then He surely thinks, so be it . . ."

Ruta watched Magda run out the cemetery gate, heading toward home. Then Ruta shuffled slowly away, each step more difficult than the last. She stopped for just a moment to catch her breath. Bone tired, she rested her hands on her hips. She understood such fatigue was just one more signal, a tweak from the Almighty himself; her time in this world was coming to an end. But strangely, she had no fear of dying. She had faith that Magda would tend the cemetery and pass on the stories, the truth of Krotoszyn. And, of course, she chuckled to herself, those vagabonds will have quite a surprise in store for them. She wished she could be there herself to see it!

Ruta turned slowly and looked back at the carved stones in the distance. In the vanishing light, the stones appeared to move, beckoning her home. Their pull was stronger than ever before. She thought of her thirty years tending the cemetery and was surprised that the end of this life could be so uneventful. But, she reasoned, that's how it is when you have lived for too long. No one is left in this world who understands you or appreciates your value. Ach, why waste my remaining energy entertaining such thoughts? I'll leave such philosophy for Rabbi Glussman to ponder, she told herself, and set her mind on her walk home.

As Ruta approached the town square, she saw Kristyna Hojonacki, an old nemesis, and three of her lifelong associates huddled on the street corner, their tongues wagging. The four had spent their lives in Krotoszyn tormenting Jews. What miseries were they planning now? As Ruta came close, the cohort nodded in unison. Their hate seemed to simmer from underneath their threadbare woolen coats.

"Good evening, Ruta," Krystyna said with a contemptuous smile.

Ruta smiled politely, bowed her head, and returned Krystyna's greeting. As she passed, she noticed how Krystyna held her head high, her sharp veiny nose stuck into the air, as though she was of Polish nobility. For the first time in many years, Ruta let her eyes rest on Krystyna's face, a face of a thousand wrinkles. Her gray skin was thick and rubbery. Her mouth sagged at the corners, a telltale sign of a stroke. Strands of brittle gray hair stuck out from under the scarf that was pulled snugly around her head and tied tightly under her pointed chin. Unhappiness seemed to seep from her droopy, watery eyes, eyes that revealed a lifetime of anxious, sleepless nights. The Almighty has not been kind to her, Ruta thought, but for the life she has chosen, it was the face she deserved.

Unexpectedly, Ruta felt a pang of compassion for her longtime enemy. After all, she thought, maybe in our old age we are now more like sisters. Don't our advanced years and our aches and pains make us more alike than different? Aren't we both, for that matter, anachronisms, remnants from another time? And, if the truth be told, she reasoned, at this age, aren't we both survivors?

Out of the corner of her eye, Ruta saw Krystyna lean toward her friends and say in a low, mocking voice: "Take a good look, ladies, at the last Jew in Krotoszyn. Ruta is the end of the line, and soon she will be gone, and at last the cemetery will be filled!"

Krystyna's words took Ruta's breath away, and she felt naked with humiliation. Then rage, fueled by a lifetime of miseries, formed in the deepest part of her chest and was pumped like boiling oil down her arms and legs and to her fingers and toes. The rage made her whole body tremble. Ruta's throat closed, and her knees buckled. She stopped walking. Unsteady, she took several deep breaths, trying to regain her composure. Her hands trembled as she pulled her frayed coat snuggly around her, protecting herself from another assault. At this precise moment she understood an appalling truth—in this life, and probably the next, the battle would go on and on because that kind of hate, Krystyna's kind, is bred in the bone. It would take a nudge from someone more persuasive than she to encourage direct intervention from the Almighty himself to change the order of things. And that nudge would have to come from someone of the next generation. Her time had come and passed.

A tired smile covered her gaunt face. Maybe she was the last Jew, and yes, she was on her way to the next world, but Magda would tend the cemetery and help keep the memories alive. And who knows, she thought, maybe the Almighty might be inclined to listen just a little more carefully to Magda than He listened to me. I'll leave those worries to the younger ones. I'm too old to be involved anymore in this monkey business.

She sighed. It is now my time to rest. And she knew when she went to bed that evening and turned out the lights, gone would be her fear that the truth of Krotoszyn would be buried with her. Instead, she would curl up in her warm bed for the last time, under a mountain of old moth-eaten blankets, and would finally sleep soundly, without worries, listening to the soft flutter of wings and the gentle voices of angels as they guided her into the next world. Once there she would find eternal peace among family and friends. Then Ruta took a deep breath, gathered her tiny frame, and turned and faced Krystyna and her associates. Ruta glowered at them for several moments. She felt the rebuke of the four pairs of eyes upon her. But she stood firm and continued to glare, unblinking. She thought of the lifetime of torment dished out by Krystyna and her cronies and then unleashed her rage in a flow of words: "The last Jew? The end of the line? No one left to tell the truth? Huh, that's what you think, Krystyna!"

The next morning Magda jumped from her bed. The air was icy, and she shivered as she slipped a heavy woolen sweater over her head. Once dressed, Magda grabbed the cemetery key that rested on the nightstand and placed it into her dress pocket. The key poked the side of her leg, as though a bony finger were nudging her along. The morning light filled her room with a soft glow that made the few pieces of furniture appear iridescent. Magda rushed to the kitchen, bursting to get to the cemetery and begin her work.

"Where are you off to so early?" her grandmother asked suspiciously as she stood bent over a shaky wooden table kneading a thick rubbery dough. "It usually takes an act by the good Lord himself to pry you from bed!"

Before her grandmother's words could evaporate, Magda heard her grandfather from across the kitchen. "Miss Hojonacki told me she saw you in the Jewish cemetery with old lady Singer. What kind of foolishness is that? Stay away from that old Jew. Now, mind what I say. No telling what she has got up her sleeve," the old man barked gruffly as he dipped another piece of coarse black bread into his coffee with a shaky, arthritic hand. Each time he did this, coffee spilled over the lip of the cup, staining the side of the already grimy mug.

"No telling what lies she's filling your head with. The war and the Jews—that's all that woman talks about. Nothing happened in Krotoszyn that doesn't happen in any war. The Jews weren't the only ones who suffered at the hands of the Germans and Russians. Besides, we have enough problems already without that old Jew causing us more bad luck. Stay away, I'm telling you!" he growled, and, with that, he stuffed a bulky piece of soaked, grainy bread into his toothless mouth and began chewing hungrily.

"Miss Singer's not a liar," cried Magda. "It's true; all the Jews were murdered during the war. Miss Singer even showed me the retaining wall at our church made from old gravestones the Germans stole from the Jewish Cemetery."

"That's what I mean," retorted the old man. "That old Jew is stirring up the past. Nobody wants to talk about those days. They are gone and done with. Nothing good can come of dredging up the past!"

Magda heard the plop of the dough when her grandmother threw it hard onto the flour-covered tabletop. She saw through the cloud of flour her grandmother, small eyes squeezed shut, make a cross in the air and mumble one of her many incantations.

"What kind of ideas are you teaching our Magda?" she yelled menacingly, pointing and shaking her crooked index finger at the old man. "You don't want Magda to know the truth about the war and what happened to the

Jews? You can't sweep the truth under the rug. You want that our Magda think just like you? Growing up in a world such as this is no picnic, especially when old fools talk such nonsense. Miss Hojonacki is always trying to stir the pot with her hate. Sweetheart, don't listen to your old grandfather or Miss Hojonacki. They're ghosts of the past. Don't pay them any attention at all. If you want to spend time with Miss Singer, then you have my blessing. Now go out and do whatever it is young girls do today, before I find a morning's worth of chores for you! And as for you, you stubborn old goat—"

The door slammed shut as Magda ran out the kitchen towards the cemetery, barely able to control her excitement about the work that lay ahead. As she ran along the street, she heard her grandmother shooing her grandfather out of the house. She took a deep breath, and the cold air stung her nose and grabbed her chest. Only in the early mornings could she smell such fresh, perfumed air, and it made her tingle all over. She reviewed in her mind exactly what she must do at the cemetery that day: pick up litter, trim back the ferns that had grown around the stones, water the lilies Miss Singer had planted. There was no time to waste. What had Miss Singer said? "Besides tsuris, one thing in Poland you can be sure about is that in spring, wild flowers paint the cemetery in a bouquet of colors." I'll get everything done before Miss Singer comes, Magda thought as she crossed the grassy field that was adjacent to the cemetery. Off in the distance she saw the tall steeple of the Catholic church, its white cross towering like a sentry against the blue sky. A short distance away, barefoot peasant boys, with powerful, squat bodies outfitted in knee-length shorts, eyed her curiously as they tended a few shaggy sheep.

When she came to the cemetery gate, Magda extracted the key from the folds her dress. The morning light illuminated the gray stones, and the dew on the grass shimmered and danced about.

As Magda put the key into the rusted lock, she saw in the distance the shapes of four men lounging against several of the stones, litter strewn around them.

"What kind of mishegas is going on here?" yelled Magda as she pushed through the gate. Her words, Miss Singer's words, came in a torrent, without any thought.

Startled by Magda's shrill voice and disoriented from their long night of drinking, the men leapt to their feet and raced to gather their possessions, mostly half-empty wine bottles and old blankets.

"Here comes the old Jew! She's at the gate. I hear that miserable voice of hers."

"Let's have a little fun with the old witch!" the fattest and most inebriated of the men yelled to his drinking companions, grinning gleefully as he planned his tricks.

Seeing Magda in the distance, the scrawniest of the quartet, disheveled from the long, eventful night, his stringy hair hanging in his eyes, groaned, "May God have mercy on our souls. The old witch has turned herself into a young woman. Run for your lives!"

"The witch has transformed herself so she can better terrorize us," another yelled as he stumbled closely behind, his round, bald head glistening and pounding from the night's festivities, a half-empty wine bottle stuck in his coat pocket.

"It's the evil eye; that's what it is, the evil eye! The old Jew is going to cast a spell and do unspeakable things to us," the youngest of the bunch cried as he pulled his pants over his flabby belly so he could better flee.

"We can't even rest in peace. What's this world coming to when a group of law abiding gentleman can't sit and trade stories and hoist a few mugs," the fat one snapped indignantly as he limped away as quickly as he could from the charging Magda.

All four men grabbed, yanked, and pushed each other as they scrambled to scale the barbed wire fence. Magda could hear their screeching as one by one they caught themselves on the barbs. Their yelps filled the air.

"If it's a spell you want, then you've come to just the right place!" yelled Magda as she approached the fence. "I'll give you more than the evil eye. I'll give each of you something to remember me by, a swift, well-aimed kick in the tuchas. That's what I'll do."

Magda could hear the men moaning as they rattled across the field toward the road. She watched them disappear into the distance. Magda sat down heavily on the bench, trying to catch her breath, her heart pounding from the excitement. The old bums!

"Stay away if you know what's good for you!" she yelled before getting up to begin her work.

Exhausted from the long day's work, Magda sat on the bench and closed her eyes, wondering what had kept Miss Singer away. She felt ill at ease in the cemetery without her friend. A cold, damp silence blanketed everything. A mist rose like a spirit from between the scattered stones. Magda shivered and rubbed her arms to warm herself. Her stomach rumbled with hunger, and Magda realized she had not eaten all day. She knew she should go home at once, but what had Miss Singer told her many times over the months? The gatherings happen at night. That's when everyone appears, after the sun goes down, when the cemetery and the streets in Krotoszyn are deserted.

Magda peered curiously about the cemetery but saw nothing unusual, no movement at all except for the scattered poplar and sycamore trees swaying and creaking in the wind, like old davening Jews. Maybe, she thought, that's what happens when you are old and lonely. You see what you want to see. Three plump pigeons perched on Rabbi Glussman's stone and cooed softly. Magda watched their small gray heads bob in all directions, as though searching in the mist.

Suddenly, Magda heard fluttering, and in an instant the pigeons vanished, and from somewhere in the far corner of the cemetery, she heard voices.

Could it be those bums have returned?

Slowly, she inched toward the muffled voices, straining to see through the fading gray light until she could make out the shadowy figure of an old man. For a moment she simply stared. Surely she wasn't hallucinating. She rubbed her eyes just to be sure. It was Rabbi Glussman. She was sure of it. He was just as Miss Singer had described—tall and gaunt, bushy white eyebrows framing sad, introspective eyes. A black skullcap rested askew on the crown of his head. His thin nose zigzagged down a narrow, pockmarked face. Side curls blended into the flowing white beard that hung to his chest. His black linen coat, buttoned to his chin and dotted with lint, extended to his ankles. A gray muffler, as old and ragged as he, was wrapped several times around his scrawny neck. He grasped in his bony fingers a worn prayer book. "Ah," the rabbi cried, looking around the cemetery, "the flowers this spring are more beautiful than ever before."

Then the ground seemed to quake and rumble, and all at once the cemetery came alive with those long departed, magically emerging from behind each stone. They huddled in small groups, some chatting about their families, others debating and disagreeing. Some pranced and sang and still others moaned and groaned, thumping their chests rhythmically, lamenting their lifetime of tsuris, while a boisterous group of boys, their side curls swinging across their faces, sang joyous songs as they danced about. A cacophony of sound filled the air.

Magda saw Pinkus Eisen, Lida Arenfeld, and Sonia Zemel circle the rabbi, seeking his counsel. Sonia, old and bent, complained bitterly, as she had in the previous world, of her son Yitzak's bachelorhood.

"The single life, whether it's in this world or the other, is a scandal," she yelped. "And for an eternity sits the lovely

Esther, a healthy specimen of a girl from a pious family, a gift from the Almighty himself, and my son the lummox doesn't make his move. All day and night he sits with his book, doesn't lift his eyes from the page. Even Bertha the marriage broker has given up! She said it was more likely she could part the Red Sea than find a match for that son of mine. It's going to take more than just a nudge from the Almighty himself to get that boy off his tuchas."

Others who had long ago departed Krotoszyn for the next world also gathered around Rabbi Glussman, listening to Sonia's tale of woe. Several old women with covered heads, shawls draped over their shoulders, listened with half-closed eyes. Pious old men, stooped over crooked wooden canes, wearing fur hats and long black coats buttoned to their chins, half listened as they conducted the day's business.

Magda inched closer, trembling at the sight unfolding before her.

"Ach, who can count on the younger ones, even in this place, to do the right thing?" announced Gustav, shaking his head and clicking his tongue. "The lack of respect for tradition was born in the other world and is nurtured here. It's shameful! The young ones want nothing more than to play their little games," he charged, peering at the group gathered around and anticipating the inevitable debate.

"I am being too harsh, you say. Just look at the boys who would rather run and kick a ball than study sacred passages. And the girls! If it's possible, they're even worse. You've seen how they prance shamelessly like Polish peasants, just to be seen! What they need to taste is a dose of my medicine," he said, puffing his chest boastfully.

Several in the group grumbled in agreement, nodding. Then Reichl, a short, round woman, overwhelmed with worry, piped in, "You think you've got tsuris? For my son, Abraham, the holy books aren't good enough—not for the modern one who goes hatless with his fancy short-waisted coat! No, only love stories written by French heretics are good enough for him. For my son the freethinker, everyday is a holiday. I could fill a scroll with the tsuris I've suffered!"

"The tsuris you've suffered," Mendel the peddler blurted out. "Benjamin, my eldest, tried to swipe my seat at the head of the dinner table last night." Those present gasped and shook their heads to hear of such disrespectful behavior.

Rabbi Glussman, who had attempted several times to get a word in edgewise, finally lost patience and shouted.

"Everyone listen! Later we can kvetch about marriages and our children, but now I have important news. Ruta is finally coming home," he said through his great white beard, his voice crackling with excitement.

"Wonderful, just wonderful," exclaimed Lida Arenfeld, adjusting the fur collar that framed her moon face and multiple chins, her almond eyes flashing with excitment. "We must prepare for her a banquet. Such a mitzvah Ruta has performed, and faithfully for so many years!" she exclaimed theatrically. Lida, who spent much ill-conceived time singing in her previous life, continued this practice, and, if possible, with even more enthusiasm and belief in her own talent. But her excessive practice yielded no better results, much to the torment of those unfortunate departed souls within hearing distance.

"Of course, it will be necessary for me to sing a medley of Sabbath songs to bless Ruta's arrival. And please don't try to talk me out of it. It is no trouble for me to perform this mitzvah. Oh, yes, our celebration must be accompanied by the gift of voice. A gift given by the Almighty himself!" Then, without any warning to those around her, she flung out her arms as though she were performing in a great concert hall and began her off-key humming in a futile attempt to loosen her always constricted throat.

Grimacing at the shrill notes that sounded like the filings of Yankel, the burly blacksmith, the rabbi wiped the sweat from his brow and strained to choose just the right words for this delicate predicament. The thought of listening to another solo performance from the tone-deaf Lida left him dizzy and weak in the knees.

"Lida, of course you will sing the sweet songs of the Sabbath," the rabbi offered diplomatically. "Such melodies the ear rarely hears! But with such an ethereal voice as yours, one that warms even the coldest of hearts, such a voice as this begs for other, less unique voices as a backdrop so that we can best appreciate your extraordinary gift. I'll assemble our choir for this important event!"

"And not only can we look forward to this upcoming performance," added Pinkus Eisner, the half-blind tailor who lost an eye in the previous world to an enraged customer in a billing dispute, "our Ruta found a young girl to care for our home. Someone to help us for years to come!"

Pinkus, short, stooped, and disheveled with a tangled, unkempt beard, was the rabbi's sexton in the previous world and was always just an arm's length away from the rabbi, poised to do his bidding. Laughing with delight and flicking the long ash of his ever-present cigarette onto the front of his threadbare coat, the rotund old man wheezed in his raspy, tobacco-harsh voice, "And with the chutzpah of that girl, God help those vagabonds should they decide to return."

"And, of course, for all she has done, Ruta will have the honor of saying the blessing over the candles," intoned Rabbi Glussman, his sonorous voice carrying over the noisy chatter. "I suggest we prepare everything Ruta enjoys. Dvorah? Dvorah Twersky, where are you when we need you?" the rabbi called impatiently, pirouetting gracefully, searching for the absent woman. "It was the same in the other world; she was never around when you needed her," the rabbi complained.

Suddenly Dvorah appeared, wiping her fleshy hands on the stained white apron that was tightly drawn across her square frame.

"Dvorah, where have you been? Time is short. You must begin the preparations for our celebration," urged the rabbi. "Ruta has come home!"

"Where have I been, Rabbi?" Dvorah said in a huff, shaking her head. "In the kitchen cooking, that's where I've been. Today should be different? Just where do you think all the meals come from? Everyone can't just sit around and schmooze all day and night. Even here, rabbi, believe it or not, meals don't appear magically. As you so often say in your sermons: 'God helps those who help themselves.' Yes, I heard; Ruta has finally come home! Of course I will prepare the Sabbath meal. Just stay out of my kitchen, and I'll prepare a feast that is fitting for so important an occasion. We will welcome her just as we welcome the Shabbat bride. No less does our Ruta deserve."

Magda stood on the edge of the cemetery, utterly bewildered, not daring to say a word. In the midst of all the confusion, she heard the excited, unfettered voices of children playing in the far corner of the cemetery. Magda crept forward. And just at the top of the hill she saw her—a tall, thin girl who seemed to float, she moved so effortlessly. It had to be Rivka! A thin white sash divided her simple blue dress at her pencil-thin waist. Her long black hair was tied by a ribbon and hung unruly down her back. Rivka just stood, gazing at Magda with soft, warm eyes.

Magda walked out of the cemetery, lifting her face to the evening stars, shiny beads of light dotting a black canvas. It was just as Miss Singer had said. The line separating earth and the mysteries of the heavens is blurred, and both worlds exist side by side. She hurried to a narrow street crowded with small, ramshackle wooden houses. Light spilled from the dirty, uncovered windows and illuminated the street with a dull glow. She saw in the windows weary peasant women and their rosy-cheeked daughters scurrying to and fro, preparing for the evening meal. From one house in the middle of the block, laughter spilled onto the street, while just two houses away, angry words between father and son were carried by a gust of wind, a prelude to the violence to come.

Magda slowed her walk as she approached the corner house, Miss Hojanaki's house. A rickety fence bordered the property. The broken gate hung ajar, useless. A washed-out yellow light seeped from the front window and mysteriously drew her forward. Magda inched onto the porch, then cautiously peeked in through the cloudy window and stole a glimpse of Krystyna wrapped in a brown blanket, slumped in her chair. She sat alone in the sparsely furnished room rocking back and forth. A single dull, yellow bulb, the only light in the room, illuminated a large wooden cross that hung crookedly on the wall directly behind the old woman. The room looked like an old, vacant church; gray shadows danced on the bare, cracked walls.

An owl perched in a sycamore tree next to the house hooted; its eerie sound disturbed the silence. Miss Hojonacki's bony hand shot out from underneath the blanket, and she pulled it tightly around her. Fear momentarily twisted her face, and she hunched her shoulders like a begger bracing for the long, cold night ahead. The old woman was skin and bones, and her vacant eyes were focused somewhere in the distance; her face sagged and fell onto her chest. The angel of death seemed to accompany her as she sat alone that evening. It was as though she finally realized her time on this earth was drawing to a close and that there may be an accounting for her lifetime of choices. She feared who would greet her when she crossed over to the next world.

Magda shifted her weight; a ghostly creak rose from a loose floorboard. The old woman snapped to attention, stuck her nose in the air, and moved her head back and forth like a bloodhound tracking a scent. Terrified by the metamorphosis of the old woman, all Magda's instincts told her to run away. But she stood frozen, unable to move. She saw Miss Hojonacki's face twitch with suspicion as she inched forward to the edge of her seat. Her misshapen hands gripped the arms of her chair. Finally, with great effort, Magda tore her eyes away, as though breaking a spell, and bolted through the gate and up the street into the darkness.

Magda reached home and stood at the front door and tried to catch her breath. Her head pounded; her face was flushed and sweaty in spite of the cold. She shuddered as she tried to rid herself of the frightening image of Miss Hojonacki. Miss Singer was right. In a world such as this, life can be topsy-turvy, with a nasty little surprise around every corner. With vagabonds, demons, and dybbukim playing their tricks, sometimes in concert with one another, a person has to be on her toes. And if it's not them, just as Miss Singer warned, it's the Almighty himself who tugs at our strings, making certain we understand our place in the big scheme of things.

Magda peeked through the grimy window and saw her grandfather wrapped in an old blanket, dozing in his wooden rocking chair. His wiry body seemed lost in the folds of the blanket. She saw his lips move in silent conversation and then smack and pucker as though he'd just finished a helping of his favorite dish—pierogis stuffed with sauerkraut. Across the room, her grandmother prepared the evening table. Her scarf was tightly drawn beneath her narrow chin; two threadbare sweaters and a pair of woolen leggings protected her from the chill of the evening. Two stubby candles in glass holders sat in the middle of the table, ready for lighting.

Spellbound, Magda saw how much her grandmother resembled Miss Singer. In so many ways they seemed to her almost like sisters. The warmth of their sparkling eyes, their deeply lined faces, their gnarled, callused hands, still tender and warm to the touch, but most of all, their resigned acceptance of a life that hadn't worked out as they'd hoped.

Magda felt a twinge of sadness. Had other, less worn paths been chosen, had someone been able to nudge the Almighty to intervene, all of them—Miss Singer, Miss Hojonacki and her grandparents, the whole bunch—could have lived their lives as friends.

While Magda turned over these thoughts, her stomach rumbled as the aroma of her grandmother's sauerkraut engulfed her. Then, stretching to her full height and feeling older and wiser than her thirteen years, she reached for the door handle with a mischievous thought. I bet with just a little nudge from me, the Almighty himself might pull a few strings, play a few tricks, and help us make things better in this world and the next.

Who's the Old Crone?

~~~~~~~~~~~~~~~~~~~~~~~~~~~~~~~~~~~~

"Abe, who's the old crone?" asked Sybil Fine, tilting her head in the direction of the old lady who sat hunched protectively over a cup of steaming tea and a small glass of prune juice.

"Her, who knows." Abe Schwartzman shrugged, studying the disheveled woman. "She showed up two mornings ago on her cane, *schlepping* all those bags full of who knows what. And she sits like a lump of clay for hours, sizing up the place, just like she's moved in. And the red *babushka*—it never comes off."

"I don't remember seeing her in the neighborhood. Maybe the poor thing is homeless?" Sybil said in a pained whisper, smoothing her blue silk suit and absentmindedly turning her diamond earring.

"I should be so homeless," countered Schwartzman as he warmed Sybil's coffee. "Both mornings the old lady paid with brand new fifties, from a bundle of them, held together with a gold money clip—the newest, crispiest bills I've ever seen, straight from the mint." Schwartzman, a florid, husky man with slightly stooped shoulders and a round, clean-shaven face, flushed with childlike glee as he contemplated the prospect of handling another crisp, fifty-dollar bill. "And can this little one pack it away," he continued, shaking his shiny bald head. "You've never in your life seen such eating! Yesterday, it was eighteen dollars and seventy-five cents worth of lox, bagels, chopped liver, and gefilte fish. And then, believe it or not, she topped it off with a dish of my plum pudding. If all my customers ate like her, I could retire in a year. All night I prayed for a restaurant full of customers with appetites just like hers."

"Well," Sybil said, "she certainly has a presence—a noble, aristocratic air about her."

"Huh! Don't be fooled. The old lady has the disposition of a Cossack and eats like one too."

"Nonsense. She's probably just lonely. I think I'll invite her to join me for a cup of tea . . ."

"I don't recommend it," Schwartzman warned, "this little one packs heat. I tried to make small talk, but I couldn't get a civil word out of her."

Sybil peered across the room and saw the woman leaning to one side like an ancient, crumbling headstone in some remote, forgotten graveyard.

As though sensing Sybil's scrutiny, the old woman looked up from her plate, blinked, and returned Sybil's searching gaze.

Startled, Sybil turned away quickly and said to Abe, "Anyway, the poor thing fits right in with your regulars. Schwartzman's Nosh looks more and more like the Jewish Home for the Aged, not one customer who's normal and under the age of eighty, other than me. Abe, you need new, young customers who spend money or your business will disappear as fast as a plate of your walnut rugelach."

She surveyed a group of three old men, the only other customers in the place, huddled together with covered heads at a booth in the far corner, all remnants from the Romanian synagogue, bankrupt and boarded up years ago. Now, with no place for them to go, the octogenarians arrived early each morning and stayed for several hours—sipping tea, noshing on the cheapest fare, and kibbitzing about spiritualism and life after death, debates that frequently drifted into polemical arguments concerning the metaphysics of Spinoza and Kant. Though generous with their opinions, when it came to money each one was more frugal than the next, and each had a knack for consuming great quantities of Schwartzman's tea while nibbling a single bagel over the course of several hours.

And what a group they were: Rabbi Fiddleman, an intense and precise man who was prone to fits of irascibility, with impish, sparkling eyes and perfectly formed ears that seemed a gift from the Almighty himself. Unfortunately, as sometimes happens in this life, when the Powers That Be decide to have a laugh at our expense, someone pays a dear price. In this case, it was the rabbi who was the butt of the heavenly joke—Fiddleman's ears were all show, only the left one retained any acuity, which forced him to cock his head awkwardly to the right and thrust his left ear forward to hear a word anyone said. Many of his former congregants surmised that this difficult and taxing maneuver accounted for the rabbi's periodic crankiness. Rabbi Fiddleman was a scholar of the old school; he was exacting in his application of Jewish law but rendered his opinions with a just and kind heart. Thus, his judgments, as well as his advice, which he dispensed liberally, were accepted by his followers without grumbling. The rabbi always wore a silk kippah atop his closely cropped gray hair and tzitzit under his dusty jacket and held court each day in Schwartzman's with his two followers—Pincus Eisenberg and Mendel Nachman.

Eisenberg, Rabbi Fiddleman's loyal sexton for over fifty years, could always be found at Fiddleman's left shoulder. This gave Eisenberg unfettered access to the rabbi's best, only half-deaf ear, which he filled with a continuous series of complaints. Pinkus was nicknamed the Kvetch, a moniker he earned when he was just a toddler in Brasov, Romania. The then colicky Pinkus, named after his father's father according to tradition, was descended from a long and distinguished line of rabbinical scholars and, considered a child prodigy by his doting parents, was expected to surpass the accomplishments of his erudite predecessors. One morning, the toddler Pinkus, still at his mother's breast at a year and a half, was observing the world from his cradle and exhibiting early, telltale signs of his lifelong cynicism—a furrowed brow and piercing stare. It was from this cradle that Pinkus uttered his first words. As the story goes, Pinkus, on that cold, dreary morning, was holding his ample belly and groaning from his crib, making every effort to persuade his frazzled mother to come and feed him. But, distracted by her many household duties, she took longer than usual to respond to the increasingly hungry and impatient Pinkus. Finally, her hands free, the harried mother approached with loving, outstretched arms to gather up the now apoplectic child. Pinkus furrowed his brow, puckered his pudgy lips, and moaned his very first words to his astonished and proud mother, "Oy vey . . . what took so long?" And the Kvetch was born.

For the next eighty plus years, complaints rolled off his tongue: "There's not enough onion in my chopped liver," he would wail at Schwartzman as he devoured great quantities of the special recipe. "What, no heat . . . it's so cold," he would sniffle to anyone close at hand as he shivered in his seat with his fedora pulled down to his ears, his overcoat collar turned up, and his gold-rimmed pince-nez perched on the tip of his red, dripping nose. "The borscht . . . not enough cream," he would belch after gulping prodigious quantities of the chilled soup, and so on. It was said the brainy Eisenberg could kvetch fluently in seven languages. That the rabbi still befriended the touchy sexton and endured with a stiff upper lip Eisenberg's grousing over the many years was testimony to Rabbi Fiddleman's patience, his unbending faith in a Supreme Power, and, most importantly, his ever-increasing deafness.

The third, and no less colorful, member of the breakfast club was Mendel Nachman. A notably small man, Nachman had a long, prestigious career as cantor at the Romanian synagogue. Because of his powerful and perfectly pitched voice, at one time Nachman was mentioned in the same breath as the great Yossele Rosenblatt. "How can such a small man have such a powerful voice?" everyone asked after hearing the diminutive Nachman sing. "Such a big voice coming from such a small man is proof the Almighty graced Nachman with a special blessing," was the obvious answer.

On festivals and holidays, Jews from every part of the city packed into every available corner of the shul to hear the master and sat transfixed as they listened with tightly closed eyes, absorbing the rich baritone coming from the resplendent Nachman. His powerful voice would spill into the street, and anyone who happened by was drawn into the overcrowded synagogue to see for themselves who brought forth such music. As he sang, Nachman's face glowed like a Sabbath candle. Women in particular singled out the bachelor Nachman for effusive praise and listened to his songs with nothing short of rapture.

But now Nachman's light was extinguished, and he sat depressed each morning in Schwartzman's, rarely uttering a sound. The master of song had become mute.

What happened to the cantor?

Nachman's gradual decline began almost two years before the synagogue was closed. After fifty years of professional singing, he began to struggle to hit the high notes, notes that before he had found with ease. At first, Nachman shrugged it off and attributed his difficulty to the onset of a cold. "After all, didn't the Festival of Lights arrive at a time of the year when everyone was coughing and sneezing?" he reassured himself while sipping gallons of hot tea, gargling glass after glass of salt water, and wrapping his neck with warm towels to soothe his throat. The hope that his problem was temporary, that it would be only a matter of time, just a few days really, before he would be at his best once again, gave Nachman some comfort. But then, much to his horror, he found that he struggled to hold notes. His breathing, once controlled and deep, the source of his powerful sound, now felt erratic and shallow. His once richly layered voice was shrill and thin as parchment. This decline left him despondent. The cantor's confidence melted away like ice in spring.

Over the next several months, things for Nachman went from bad to worse. As his voice diminished week by week, Nachman became more and more desperate. He spent his days in his small, richly furnished apartment pacing with worry and practicing for hours. But no matter the amount of practice, he continued his steady decline. Then, one day, Miss Hepenheimer, the dried-up old bitty who lived two doors down, rapped on his door. The old lady, with a bony, masculine face and a low, coarse voice to match, immediately lit into Nachman, brandishing two knitting needles and snarling about the "off-key warbling" that grated on her nerves, making the short time she had left in this life a living hell. Nachman, too stunned to respond, stood mute in the doorway holding his teacup, his throat swathed in warm towels, until the old woman wearied and, after one last menacing shake of a knitting needle, took her leave.

"Everyone's a critic," he muttered to himself.

The distraught Nachman turned to prayer, petitioning for direct intervention from the Almighty himself. After all, he pleaded on bent knees, hadn't he always used his gift unselfishly and taken care to bring the Almighty's sacred music to all those who cared to listen? And was he not, he further pointed out, always devout and charitable? In his efforts to curry divine favor, Nachman became so obsessed with giving thanks to the Almighty that not only did he say the required blessings before and after each meal, he also said a blessing over each morsel of food he placed into his mouth. Still, Nachman's voice failed to improve, and mealtimes, once a great source of pleasure for the cantor, became interminable, joyless events.

Then the demons of melancholy arrived and became his constant companions, torturing his soul. His once cheerful personality turned sour, and the pink faded from his drawn cheeks. Overnight it seemed the cantor's great black beard, which hung to his belt, had turned white. Before his troubles began, Nachman would respectfully whisper a prayer of thanks for his gift before he sang a note. But now angry words replaced the prayerful thanks. "What kind of God plays such tricks?" was his frequent refrain. "What have I done to deserve such shabby treatment?" he bitterly complained.

Congregants, of course, noticed Nachman's decline. The cantor who once sang so effortlessly now strained, grimaced, really, as he tried to complete the service. The once impervious cantor now sweated profusely from the strain, sometimes soaking through his fine silk shirt and dark jacket. Congregants struggled to concentrate on their prayers as they listened to the pained cantor. At first, his admirers were understanding and quick with consoling words. "Didn't all great artists have their bad days? Was every story written by the great Sholem Aleichem a masterpiece?"

But over the months, patience wore thin, and the mood in the synagogue shifted. Attendance dwindled. Women, once his most ardent supporters, went so far as to complain to the rabbi. A few of the bolder women, mostly the rich, idle wives of the board members, asked, "Aren't there young cantors, recent graduates, who could bring a new, fresh voice?" Such a change, they further asserted, would actually benefit Cantor Nachman, as it would provide him a "well-deserved retirement."

But Rabbi Fiddleman wouldn't hear of it and stuck by his friend of almost fifty years. Thus, the cantor retained his position until the day the synagogue became insolvent and closed its doors for the last time. Since that day, almost ten years ago, Rabbi Fiddleman continued to keep an eye out for the melancholic cantor, making sure he paid his bills, maintained a clean, well-ordered wardrobe, and ate balanced meals to keep his strength up.

"How about another schmear of cream cheese for my good friend Nachman, at no extra cost, of course . . . ," Fiddleman would announce to the waitress. Nachman, as though he were jolted out of a stupor, would raise his head and turn his pale face, which had not seen the sun in a very long time, and sigh in a weak, barely audible voice, one that retained the cadence of one who had once lived in Jassy, Romania, "Yes, I suppose a little schmear would be nice . . ."

Silently he would sit, detached and slumped in his chair, reminiscing about the days when audiences stood in line for hours to purchase tickets to his performances, how the women would gather around to bask in his shining light. Each day, sitting in Schwartzman's, he would bitterly lament the way his gift had been unceremoniously snatched away by the very powers that once favored him. Nachman learned, as do all mortals who are blessed with extraordinary abilities, that such gifts are merely on loan and are never permanent . . .

"Speaking of young customers, where is that daughter of yours?" Schwartzman asked Sybil, hoping the young woman would arrive famished and, as usual, contribute to his financial security by ordering her typical Friday breakfast—an expensive feast of potato pancakes, a double order of cherry blintzes with mounds of whipped cream, a cheese strudel, and a chocolate phosphate to wash it all down.

Sybil Fine peered out the floor-to-ceiling window and searched through the hustle and bustle on the street outside. She took an anxious breath and grimaced with worry. "That daughter of mine is always late, never on time for anything. Where could she be? I don't know what I'm going to do with her."

"Has Dina found a job yet?" Abe asked.

"No, and I'm not sure she's even looking. I've tried to

interest her in my business, but she refuses to even consider it. This life never stops with the disappointments.
God answers my prayers and blesses me with a daughter
but, for reasons only He knows, gives me an obstinate
one who can't tell time! It's one aggravation after another,"
she sighed, shaking her head and frowning. A number
of fine creases, extending downward from the corners of
her delicate lips, stood out against her otherwise smooth,
flawless skin. Sybil picked up her coffee cup and noticed
dried food crusted on the lip. "Abe," she said pointing an
accusing index finger at the dirty spot, "your dishes aren't
so clean this morning." The glossy red nail polish made her
long tapered finger into a blood-tipped sword.

"That damn Slotkin," Schwartzman cried, shaking his
head. "I've got a new meshuga dishwasher. Out of nowhere
he appeared looking for a job. He's worked only two days,
and already I've got tsuris with this one. But what can I
expect hiring a Hasidic dishwasher who thinks he's the
next Maimonides. The boychik's too busy memorizing
every word of the Talmud to wash a dish or two. That's
what I get for having a heart of gold and doing a mitzvah.
My ex-wife complained that with my disposition I should
have been a social worker." That said, the heavy-boned
Abe Schwartzman whirled like a ballerina and rushed full
tilt towards the kitchen. In his frantic rush, Abe caught a
glimpse of Magic McKnight casually leaning against the
wall at the far end of the room. "Magic! What? I'm paying
you to lounge around? Bus tables, wash windows . . . do
something," Schwartman ordered as he advanced toward

the kitchen. Always solicitous of his paying customers, Abe came to a screeching halt at the table of the strange old woman. Before the fawning Schwartzman could ask about her corned beef and chopped liver sandwich and offer her a side of noodle kugel, the old woman looked up with a yellow, strained face—the prune juice had not yet produced its desired effect—and, fondling the remnant of her sandwich, coughed, drew a labored breath, and wheezed in a thick Yiddish accent, "Shmutz, shmutz . . . on my cup there's shmutz. What kind of place am I sitting that serves shmutz?"

The near-sighted Schwartzman, gasping from exertion, his blue eyes bulging behind thick, wire-rimmed glasses, his bald, globe-like dome glowing crimson and filled with visions of an emaciated and inert Slotkin, his feet propped up, reading, and munching a freshly baked knish amongst stacks of unwashed dishes, raced at breakneck speed for the kitchen door. "Slotkin, what do you think this is, a shul?" he screeched as he shoved open the swinging doors. "Freeloader! Swindler! How many times do I have to tell you? Stop studying and get off your tuchas and wash dishes for once. Elbow grease, give it elbow grease . . ."

Still leaning against a far wall with a dishtowel hanging smartly from his belt and a serving tray held firmly in his confident grasp, Magic McKnight, Schwartzman's busboy of two years, turned to his new assistant, Jermain Jacks, winked, and chuckled with delight as he watched Abe disappear into the kitchen. At six feet three and two hundred and twenty pounds of sculpted muscle, Magic towered over the diminutive Jermain.

"Slotkin is a gift from heaven, my friend—a gift! As long as fat-man Schwartzman is fussing at that skinny religious fanatic we won't have to lift a finger; we are free, *mon*, home free!" Magic said in his newly acquired Jamaican accent. This metamorphosis may have been a first in the annals of linguistic history, as there was no documented evidence that Magic had ever spent one minute on Jamaican soil or, for that matter, anywhere else outside the three-mile radius of his birthplace on Lenox Avenue.

With his nemesis Schwartzman safely decamped to the kitchen, the jubilant Magic puffed out his chest like a peacock and announced, "Now, my friend, it's time to celebrate our good fortune and watch Magic do his magic." With that, Magic took a deep breath, closed his eyes for just a moment as though praying for strength, and raised his tray with his mighty right arm and held it high over his head. Using a series of complex motions, he turned his arm and wrist as he spun the heavy tray round and round on his fingertips. The tray hummed as it spun, picking up more and more speed as though powered by a supernatural force. Jermain watched in wonderment. Magic swayed his muscular torso rhythmically as he expertly balanced the whirling tray. Streaks of colored light reflected off the mountain of glasses, plates, and silverware piled high on the tray and filled the dining room with a spectacular rainbow of blues, yellows, and greens. As Magic's movements became more and more exaggerated, his toothy smile grew wide.

As if by divine intervention, everything on the tray stayed put. The entire spectacle defied all laws of physics. Then, with another flurry of creative movements, including an impressive but unusual rocking of his hips, Magic ended his feat by carefully altering the position of his fingertips, gradually slowing the spinning disk, and finally bringing it safely to rest. He bowed to his appreciative assistant. His feat of artistry, balance, and exuberance was a marvel to behold. Magic grinned, a look of self-satisfaction, a swagger, really, that all experts have when they are at the top of their game and believe things will never change. So, with the confidence of a man who felt his place in the world was secure, Magic looked around the restaurant with a cocky smile that said, "If you think that was something, just you wait . . ."

"Amazing," Jermain gushed, "but what's with the accent? You're not Jamaican."

"Mon, the islands are in my blood. I should have been born in Jamaica. All I can figure, the Cat upstairs is playing a practical joke on me. But one day, mon, I'll be where I belong. Huh, do you think the Magic Man is going to bus tables for Schwartzman the rest of his life? No way, mon; there's money to be made in the islands. And Magic is going to make his share and lead the good life. Oh yes, the islands are in my blood . . ."

"Where've you been? I've been waiting over half an hour!" Sybil Fine cried as Dina lumbered into a seat across the table from her mother. The young woman said nothing but rolled her eyes and reached hungrily for a menu; streaks of cold, broken light escaped the sky's thick blanket of clouds and illuminated and exposed the two women for a moment. Dina puffed heavily, catching her breath. She wore a wrinkled jumpsuit that fit much too snuggly; the buttons down the front strained and were close to bursting. The young woman's plump body had no angles or edges, only smooth, swollen curves. Her face was oval, with puffy cheeks and a small afterthought of a nose. She wore no makeup, and her thick, black, curly hair was unruly. Sybil's eyes moved from her daughter's detached, placid face to her jumpsuit— a garish garment of bold red and blue horizontal stripes, tied at the waist with a yellow sash.

"Again, it's the red and blue stripes; I've told you count-less times, you're not a girl who should wear bold stripes. They're just not flattering . . ."

Dina's entire bearing was aloof and impenetrable, like one who considers herself to be just passing through, who safely views life through a key hole, a bystander to its events.

"Mother, would you just stop. I'm twenty-two; I'll wear what I want. Besides, who do I have to impress, anyway?"

"What I'm telling you is, make yourself presentable. You never know who you might meet. Anyway, for once have a little patience with me. You think it's been easy raising you without your poor father? God in all his wisdom gives me a first-rate husband with a third-rate heart; in this life the Almighty gives with one hand and, like a thief, snatches away with the other. You go figure the sense that makes."

"Why do you always bring up Dad's death? It's morbid.

I don't want to keep hearing about his arteriosclerosis."

"Don't talk fresh to your only mother, who, I might add, has worked her fingers to the bone for you."

"Here we go again, the guilt trip," scoffed Dina as she studied the menu carefully, planning a culinary extravaganza.

Sybil remained silent for a moment, observing her daughter, and then said protectively, "Dina, go easy on the fried foods and the kugel; remember what happened to your poor father. I don't want that for you."

"I'm fat . . . I've accepted that."

"I didn't say you're fat. You're zaftig . . . There's a difference."

"Not to me."

"Well, you're zaftig; Jewish men like zaftig, just remember that."

Dina scowled.

"Don't give me that look. I'm your mother, and if I say you're zaftig, you're zaftig; case closed!" Then, pointing and shaking her tapered finger at Dina, Sybil added: "What you need, young lady, is somebody to care about."

Dina glared, her anxious face moving into the light. "It's not going to happen. So stop talking about it."

"Ach, such cynicism. Mothers must pass it to their daughters, because when I was your age I felt the same way. I didn't think I'd meet anyone either, until I met your father, that is. Then everything changed."

"How nice for you. But what does that have to do with me?"

"Because when you least expect it, you'll meet someone, and you'll know he's the one as soon as you look into his eyes. And you better be ready because whoever orchestrates such things can be impatient and may not give you a second chance."

"How did you know Dad was the right one?" Dina asked, curiosity softening her voice.

"Do you want the long or short version?"

"What do you think?"

"All right, then, the short one: I remember the night like it was yesterday. I was just about your age and was out to dinner with your Aunt Rose at Morshevsky's; you know the place. It's had more facelifts than cousin Sherry. We went every Thursday night for the pastrami special. Old man Morshevsky was a great artist in the kitchen. He prepared his pastrami like your grandmother, the Romanian way; he used goose marinated for weeks in a special brine. I can still taste it."

"Get to the point," Dora snapped.

"That night I was enjoying my pastrami sandwich and listening to your Aunt Rose when I happened to look up, and I saw your father staring at me from across the room. He was wearing a wrinkled, threadbare shirt under a ragged jacket with a Yiddish newspaper sticking out of one pocket. He was completely rumpled. And not only that, he was short and stocky—not the type I usually fell for. But your father had such a friendly, playful face. And the smile! Oh my God, it brightened everything around him. As soon as I saw him, I knew he was the one. It was rockets, horns, and fireworks, with all the colors, exploding at the same time. We couldn't take our eyes off each other. I could barely sit still, but that aunt of yours just kept talking. I didn't hear a word she said the rest of the evening." Leaning closer to Dina, she continued in a whisper, "You're the only one I've ever told this to, but the way your father looked that night, I thought I was falling for a real greenhorn, one of those who only read from right to left and with no job to boot. But God works in mysterious ways. Who could have guessed he owned apartment buildings! I just sat there staring, not able to move. Let me tell you something—every night I pray you should be so lucky and meet someone as kind as your father."

"Meet someone. Fat chance. Things like that don't happen to girls who look like me," Dina said. She closed the menu, placing it carefully behind the metal napkin holder as the waitress approached to take her order.

"Don't say such things. Of course it will happen to you. Just be ready when it does . . . And remember, young lady; you're *zaftig*, and that's final."

From across the room, the old woman watched Sybil and Dina. Suddenly a vise-like cramp, a digestive catastrophe, knotted her stomach and twisted her like a pretzel. Grimacing, she lifted her bony face upward and moaned through clenched teeth, "All right, enough already. You don't have to keep reminding me—I know You're there. Be patient for once, will You? These things You ask that I do are complicated and take time. Anyway, between the constant interruptions I've suffered, who can get anything done?" Then the old woman sprang to her feet, grabbed her cane, and with short, quick steps, hurried to the bathroom . . .

Magic smiled as he watched Sybil Fine pay her bill and march out the door, leaving Dina to finish her breakfast. His eyes gleamed with caddish anticipation as he readied himself for his move.

"Magic, what do you have up your sleeve?" Jermain asked, studying his friend's mischievous eyes. "I can tell you're planning something; you've got that look."

"See that big, luscious girl sitting over there?" Magic tilted his head toward Dina. "I've watched her meet her mother for breakfast every Friday morning for a year. And let me tell you, my man, they're loaded. This girl doesn't know it yet, but she's going to have a little Magic in her life. She's going to be Magic's meal ticket out of here. Jermain, my man, now you are going to see how an expert operates with the ladies. Oh, yes," he continued as he adjusted his belt and smoothed his wrinkled pants, "now you're going to see the Magic Man work his magic."

Magic strutted the distance to Dina with the feverish energy of a gladiator. He leaned forward and, in one swift motion, scooped up her empty dishes. With a broad, confident smile, a smile that proudly showcased two gold-capped front teeth, announced, "It's the Magic Man at your service." Shaking his head, he continued in reassuring tones. "I appreciate a girl who knows how to enjoy a bit of breakfast . . ."

Dina, blushing slightly, handed Magic her half-empty coffee cup. Magic, boldly seizing his opportunity, ever so slightly brushed his calloused index finger back and forth against the inside of her wrist as he reached for the cup. Dina yanked her arm away and jerked her face upward, and her eyes, at once embarrassed and angry, met Magic's for the first time. They stared at each other for several awkward moments. Not a word passed between them, but her eyes narrowed, and her face contorted tightly into an expression that screamed, "Take a hike, you jerk."

Embarrassed and flustered by Dina's abrupt and un-expected rejection, Magic's confidence melted away, and beads of sweat formed a watery mustache on his upper lip. He shuffled backwards and tried to recover with an exag-gerated display of bluster, raising a tray high over his head with his magnificent arm. The tray, loaded with dishes, was balanced expertly on the fingertips of his right hand. Then he looked into Dina's eyes and, with an indignant snort, announced to the startled young woman, "Huh, you don't think the Magic Man is good enough? I'll show you something you won't soon forget!"

In a flash, Magic snapped his wrist, and the tray began spinning, at first slowly, then faster and faster. Magic tried to settle into his groove, but the sting of Dina's rebuke lingered, and he had difficulty concentrating on the now whirling tray. To make matters worse, Magic took his eye off the tray for just a fraction of a second, no more, but it was enough to cause a wobble. His powerful legs, the source of his uncanny balance, buckled slightly, and he stumbled. Magic's ever-present smile turned into a grimace. The sudden jingling and clanking of dishes was like a death rattle. He frantically adjusted the position of his arm and spread his fingers wider apart. But it was no use; the tray spun even faster. At that instant, Magic understood his predicament; the tray was spinning inexorably out of his control. He felt the unmistakable wave of dread that signals imminent disaster. The tray now had a mind of its own, lifting like a helicopter from the landing pad of his fingertips. Magic let out a mournful howl that sounded like the plaintive blast of a shofar as the tray soared higher and higher. Half-empty glasses, cups, and bowls began flipping and crashing in midair, and the air in the restaurant filled with thousands of multicolored liquid droplets that shimmered yellow and gold, like a fireworks display. Pieces of bread, cake, the last bits of plum pudding, and chunks of horseradish and chopped liver danced like so many puffy balloons.

Dina sat transfixed, gaping at the unfolding spectacle.

Then, as if choreographed, the twirling and tumbling assortment of dishes yielded to gravity and sped toward Swartzman's shiny tile floor. Explosions of shattering glass reverberated throughout the restaurant. Emerging from this thundering din, several knives and forks, flashing in the light, took horizontal flight in perfect formation across the restaurant, like heat-seeking missiles, toward Fiddleman, Nachman, and Eisenberg, who were hunched together over tea in their private nook. Each one was oblivious to the unfolding events, they were so absorbed in their discussion.

As the projectiles headed their way, Rabbi Fiddleman was explaining to his two skeptical friends that the Torah makes no definitive statement about an afterlife. "So," the rabbi posited as the missiles approached, "who in this world can absolutely be sure of a next?"

Eisenburg, feeling every one of his eighty-five years, didn't take kindly to the prospect of departing this life for an abyss of nothingness. He tried to stop the rabbi's erudite discourse by moaning, "Death, afterlife . . . such unpleasant topics for a Friday . . ."

Nachman, suddenly experiencing a premonition of death, turned and, much to his horror, saw the approaching projectiles now cruising at supersonic speed directly toward them. Realizing they had only a few precious seconds left to live, Nachman attempted to scream, but only a soft, insignificant, bird-like squeak emerged from the old cantor. Then, realizing he had just one more opportunity to save his friends from catastrophe, Nachman took a deep breath, prayed to the Almighty for the return of his lost voice, and bellowed at the top of his lungs, "Hit the deck!" It was a miracle. Nachman's voice shook the restaurant. The old cantor had not produced such a rich, powerful sound in many years. Another miracle— Rabbi Fiddleman heard the cantor's warning and, like a man half his age, dove headfirst underneath the table for safety. Nachman, his prayer answered, his work done, found a safe haven alongside the shaken rabbi. Eisenberg was still so busy kvetching about the distressing news that the Torah did not provide crystal clear evidence of an afterlife that he didn't hear the cantor's warning. Knives and forks, their sharp points flashing, bore down on the hapless sexton. As though nudged by an unseen hand, Eisenberg turned toward the flashes of light and gasped, choked, and pursed his lips like a carp. Fear of his impending demise held Eisenberg in its iron grip, and he sat paralyzed with dread as the projectiles whizzed by, just centimeters beneath his quivering chin, and stuck into the wall behind him.

It was over as quickly as it began, and an uneasy quiet descended over the restaurant.

A stupefied Schwartzman, who had watched the entire spectacle safely behind the cash register, didn't recognize the grim sight that was once his well-ordered restaurant: the rabbi and cantor were huddled beneath their table hugging one another for dear life; Eisenberg was a marble statue, his face chiseled into terror-stricken surprise; broken dishes and splattered food covered the floor and walls.

Schwartzman anxiously scanned the room to make sure his newest and most beloved customer, the old woman, had survived the chaos. In just a matter of seconds, however, Schwartzman came to the painful realization that she was nowhere to be seen and had, in fact, vanished into thin air without paying her bill. In a fit of rage that was fueled by the expensive prospect of replacing all of those broken dishes, Schwartzman, his round face crimson and puffed with fury, exploded, "Where's the old lady? The gonif owes me twenty-two fifty. Oy vey, I've been stiffed . . ."

Magic, who was bent over a heap of broken dishes, looked around sheepishly at the destruction and found everyone glaring at him. Mortified at the appalling and unforeseen turn of events, he threw open his mouth and, like a man possessed by demons, let out a terrible wail. "Slotkin, get out here and help clean up you son-of-a-b—" Gone was the Jamaican patois.

The terror-stricken Slotkin bounded out of the kitchen clutching a knish in one hand and a tome in the other. Dina, watching the unfolding scene with rapt attention, saw the bewildered and quaking Slotkin rush frantically toward Magic. Beads of sweat dripped from his narrow brow and disappeared into his wispy, black beard. His side curls, which hung the full length of his pale face, waved rhythmically back and forth. His pointed chin vibrated nervously.

As though ordained by an Unseen Power, Dina could not take her eyes off the disoriented dishwasher, who was now standing over the distraught Magic McKnight. The sight of the slouching, hundred-and-ten-pound Slotkin stuffing the last bit of knish into his toothy mouth and hiding his book in the waistband of his baggy black pants took Dina's breath away. It was as though she had just seen King David himself. Dina felt dizzy; butterflies flipped and flopped and fluttered their wings in her stomach. Her smile turned dazzling. For the first time in her life, feelings of joy and happiness overwhelmed her, and her heart began to pound, filling every part of her with desire. The air around her turned fragrant and sensual.

Dina's eyes, shining with light and wonder, reached out and met Slotkin's and pulled at him forcefully, not letting go. The confused young man, unworldly in such matters of the heart, was no match for the beguiling power of the zaftig Dina, and his cheeks burned with a strange, unfamiliar excitement. Dina saw a whole other world, rich with new possibilities, unfolding before her, and at that instant, just as her mother had said, she knew. Oh yes, she knew he was the one . . .

A year has come and gone since the old woman vanished without a trace from the wreckage of Schwarzman's Nosh, and the Powers That Be have not grown tired of playing mischievous tricks on those who were there that fateful day.

Just months after Magic's disaster, a radiant Dina exchanged vows with Moyer Slotkin under the wedding canopy, but not before a trembling, diffident Slotkin, hopeless at any activity that didn't involve a book, stomped erratically, hopped really, and missed the wine glass three consecutive times before he finally, with the gentle help of Rabbi Fiddleman, found his mark. Observing this spectacle, several of the old widows whispered among themselves that a man with such poor aim may not be much good to Dina in her marriage bed, as it was unlikely that Rabbi Fiddleman would be there to provide his kind assistance.

In another remarkable turn of events, Dina took a sudden interest in her mother's business. Through all those years of sitting idly and watching the world pass by, Dina had stockpiled an enormous amount of pent-up energy, which she unleashed in a dazzling display of business acumen. The result was stunning: money, barrels of it, rolled in. Thus, Moyer Slotkin was able to follow the traditions of old and concentrate fully on his Talmudic studies, never concerning himself with worldly affairs such as gainful employment.

Like her daughter, Sybil, too, fell under a magical spell and noticed something few other women saw in Abe Schwartzman. Before she knew it, she found herself under the wedding canopy with the irrepressible restaurateur. Sybil learned that on the second go-round you don't necessarily see fireworks. Oh no, the Powerful Forces that choreograph these things see to it that this dance is slow and deliberate, something like selecting a book to curl up with on a cold winter's night. You are first drawn to its cover, then you carefully mull over the title to see if it strikes your fancy. If it does, you might peruse the first few pages to see if the story sufficiently piques your interest. And if you feel in your heart the story is worthy of your attentions, then it is indeed time to get to know the author much better!

"How could such an unlikely match be possible?" the gossipmongers asked in bewildered tones. Eisenberg, who always finagles a front row seat to these tongue wagging sessions, *kvetches* just loudly enough for everyone to hear, "What kind of *mishegas* is going on around here? Everything is turning upside down!"

Then one day, out of the blue, a little *mazel* came Magic's way. The frugal Schwartzman, always with a keen eye for savings, surmised that it was cheaper to finance a move to Jamaica for his accident-prone busboy than to continually replace broken dishes, and gladly advanced the funds for a one-way ticket to Kingston.

And if all that weren't proof enough of a Higher Power with a master plan, Nachman's light began shining brightly once again. Each new day finds Miss Hepenheimer sitting in Nachman's apartment with a mountain of yarn piled on her lap. Her tiny hands, youthful once more, move effortlessly as she knits thick sweaters for Nachman to protect him from a chill. And as the twice-blessed Nachman places himself at his music stand and sings song after song, his face once more glowing like a Sabbath candle, Miss Hepenheimer, with half-closed, dreamy eyes, hums melodies in perfect harmony as the rich aroma of a sizzling brisket fills the cantor's apartment and wraps around both of them like a warm blanket. And, according to the busybodies who make it their business to know such things, Miss Hepenheimer, whose grateful face is now soft and joyful, with eyes that sparkle like diamonds, often does not emerge from Nachman's apartment for days at a time . . .

And the old crone?

For over a year her disappearance was shrouded in mystery. As time passed and memories faded, more than a few thought that maybe she had been a figment of their imagination. Then, one day, a shaken Eisenberg, his face pale, stumbled into Schwartzman's telling this tale:

"You won't believe this, but I just saw the old lady on Kensington Avenue leaning on her cane with that same red babushka tied under her chin. I tried to talk to her about the money she owes Schwartzman, but you try crossing

Kensington at lunchtime—cars, buses, trucks—oy vey, it's a racetrack out there. Who's safe walking anymore? I finally made it across and got to the curb—it was so high, I'm telling you, another Mt. Sinai! You try stepping over the damn thing quickly without breaking your ankle and who knows what else. When I finally got across I looked up again, and the strangest thing . . . she was gone, like a puff of smoke . . . I'm telling you, she just vanished into thin air, shopping bags and all. It was like trying to catch a little dream. I understand, old ladies are a peculiar lot and sometimes do strange things, but disappear? You tell me! Such a thing is just not of this world." Eisenberg picked up his teacup, took a sip, and spit it right back out. "Ach, it's like iced tea! Where are they when you need them?" Eisenberg searched for a waitress to warm his cup, his memory of the old lady already fading away like a prayer chanted in the wind. "Ten years coming to Schwartzman's and never a waitress when you need one. Is it asking too much for a waitress once in a while?" he moaned to no one in particular. "The tsuris we're made to suffer in this meshuga world . . .Oy vey, such a life."

Such a life, indeed!

Miss Bargman

"*L'chaim*," toasted Miss Bargman, her voice a mixture of Łódź, Poland, and New York's Lower East Side. Her words echoed in the cold, damp, sparsely furnished apartment. The early morning March winds made their way through her apartment windows, ruffling the once white, now yellowed lace curtains. The old woman raised and then emptied her crystal wine glass, which had traveled to America with Miss Bargman and her family over eighty years ago.

The wine was sweet, and Miss Bargman savored its fruity aftertaste. Warmth spread through her old body, an antidote to the constant, penetrating dampness of the apartment that made her bones ache. The old woman wrapped her robe tightly around her midsection and gave herself a hug, trapping the warmth around her.

"I should treat myself to another," she said softly after emptying her glass. I deserve it, she thought. I have been a very good girl. At eighty-nine years of age, I don't have the opportunity or energy to be otherwise.

Without warning, a ribbon of pain grabbed deep in her back. First she tried to ignore it, hoping it would go away.

Maybe if I sit quietly that will help, she thought. When the pain persisted, the old woman took a deep breath and carefully bent forward to loosen its grip. "Oy," the old woman groaned, such a life. Mornings are always the worst; when I wake it's always the same—pain. Then the daily ritual: first, legs and feet and toes—are they still obeying my command? Then arms and hands. Can I still point and grip? One of these mornings, sooner rather than later, things won't be so routine. After all, I won't live forever. Each day it took her longer to get out of bed. Soon my day will consist of only dressing and undressing, she thought.

"Oh, stop your kvetching," she chastised herself. What good does complaining do? I must think about something other than my aches and pains. The old woman thought of her father, how he had begun each day with a glass of wine and a toast.

"Why do you do that every day, have wine and say 'l'chaim?'" she asked her father once. "The wine makes the blood flow," he said with a laugh. "The toast, Dora, is to remind myself everyday to choose life. A good Jew, Dora, chooses life. Let me tell you something, it's written that when a Jew dies he has to account for all the good things God created that he refused to enjoy. One day you will understand this, but now we have work to do, important business. Come *puppele*, its time for our mission." And like always, he whisked her out of the apartment for an early morning walk down Delancey in search of a Yiddish newspaper.

The old woman smiled as she remembered the chaos on

the street—chattering housewives sweeping the front steps of their apartment buildings, others scrubbing windows, men scurrying to and fro, preparing for a day's work. Shouting and jostling. Entire families arguing about old scores carried all the way from the shtetls in Eastern Europe or, sometimes, just for the sport of it. Smells overwhelmed. Week-old garbage reeked in alleyways. Rotting fruit was scattered on the curbs. Freshly washed laundry hanging from clotheslines on the back porches of gray tenements lined the street and billowed in the breeze. And the newspaper vendors! All the young boys, always running to make a sale. Each pulled a dirty wagon filled with papers. They wore baggy shirts, ill-fitting pants, either too short or long, and, no matter the weather, hats pulled to their ears. The boys all looked like brothers—the same ink-stained faces and grimy hands and scratchy, defiant voices. They competed with each other, chanting the names of their respective newspapers—*Forverts, Warheit, Der Tog, Morgen Zhurnal*. Yiddish filled the air.

Miss Bargman remembered how her father would give her two pennies to buy that day's edition of *Forverts*. When she handed him the paper, her father would always say with a little laugh, "Let's see what the great Mr. Cahan has to say." Then off they would go, to their three-room flat on Delancey Street.

These things I remember, but how long has it been? The old woman calculated the number of years that had passed since she was a little girl, buying her father's newspaper for two pennies. It must have been around 1915, the year we lived on Delancey, she thought. Eighty years ago! Could it be eighty years already? All these ancient memories, and I can't recall what I had for supper yesterday. Maybe it's because I don't get enough rest. I wish just once I could sleep late. No matter what time I go to bed, I get up at the same hour. It's like I have an alarm clock in my head. When I was young, I could sleep all day. But now, each morning, I'm up at dawn.

Ach, enough of the daydreaming, the old woman thought as she rose from the kitchen table and slowly walked to her bedroom to dress. Her knees were stiff from sitting, and shooting pains traveled through her legs. She heard her slippers shuffle against the wood floor. Already an hour has passed, she thought. It's getting late. I must face the day. It's Friday, and I have things to do.

It was seven o'clock in the morning when Miss Bargman finished dressing. She came out of the bedroom wearing a white turtleneck sweater and black stretch pants pulled high over her thin waist. Underneath her sleeve on her left arm she wore several silver bracelets. A silver Star of David hung from a thin chain around her neck. A tortoiseshell clasp secured her still thick gray hair in a tightly wrapped bun on the back of her head. Meticulously applied makeup softened a network of criss-crossing lines on her narrow, bony face, and eyeliner highlighted round, black, stubborn eyes.

She entered the living room, sat on the faded green sofa, and lifted a photo album from beneath the stained coffee table. She began to breathe hard from the effort of lifting the heavy, awkward album.

Oy, everything is such a chore, she thought as she sat motionless, trying to calm her erratic breathing. I will sit and look at photographs while I wait to see if anyone telephones or comes to visit today, she told herself.

The old woman gazed around her apartment. She felt an uneasiness in the pit of her stomach. Never before had her home appeared so drab, so in need of painting and repair. It was as though she saw it clearly for the first time. Maybe the chill in the air is making me morose, she thought. Miss Bargman straightened the sleeves of her sweater and looked down at her coordinated outfit. I hope I look presentable. One must always be prepared for company, especially on Sabbath eve, she reminded herself. Someone may come, you never know.

Miss Bargman glanced at the telephone on the end table to her left. It has been so many days since it has sounded. I wonder if the ringer still works. Could the phone be disconnected? I'm sure I paid the bill this month, but with my memory . . .

Panic seized her.

She grabbed the receiver and listened to the flat buzzing of the dial tone. A chill went through her as she thought how harsh the sound was compared to the voice of a friend. Maybe today—maybe I will be lucky today and someone will call. Anything is possible, she thought, especially on the Sabbath.

Miss Bargman huddled on the soft couch and began to

turn the pages of the album. The photographs were torn and stained. She peered at an old photograph of a group of her father's friends. Staring from the photograph was Morris Blau, a man much younger than her father. Miss Bargman leaned forward, took a breath, and sighed. Her eyes traced the lines of the young man's face. It has been so long, I can't remember exactly what it was about him that was so interesting. But it was clear to me then. Oh, those blue eyes—those I remember. He always took time to talk to me. He was such a nice man. I could feel something between us, like we were kindred spirits. I think Morris felt the same; if not, why would he go out of his way to talk with me? The old woman remembered how he had abruptly stopped visiting. I know father had something to do with that. He didn't think Morris was good enough. No one ever was. I wonder what happened to him? I'm sure he married and had a family. Ach, why think about him after so many years? Such strange things I think about lately. But what else is there to entertain an old woman like me? she thought.

It was eleven o'clock, and the old woman sat at the living room window of her third floor walk-up. The sun's rays, magnified by the window glass, warmed her. She let the muscles of her body relax to allow the sun to sink deep into her. Looking around her apartment, Miss Bargman was seized by a sense of isolation. She felt detached from her surroundings, as though she didn't belong. Maybe if I had moved from this neighborhood when everyone else did, things would be different for me. She often thought of living away from the city in a small home on a tree-lined street in a quiet, friendly neighborhood. In such a place, she imagined, visitors would be plentiful. She leaned forward in her chair and parted the curtains and peered outside, searching. There was little activity on the street below or in the small, litter-strewn park across the way. Why is it so quiet on a Friday morning? Don't women shop for the Sabbath any more? she asked herself. But shop where? Everything is so different from the way it was. She thought of all her old friends who moved to the suburbs long ago and of Jewish shops now vanished. Where was Kaplin's Bakery, with its buttery pound cakes and long lines of women every Friday morning? And where was Schwartz's Five and Dime, the repository of just about everything? You name it, and Schwartz offered it for the lowest price! Where had Mr. Trackenberg and his Kosher Market gone? Lox and smoked carp sold for just twenty-five cents a pound, and pickled herrings stored in a large barrel sold for five cents each. After a day of shopping and haggling, her father would say, flushed with excitement, "See, Dora, we have Łódź in America!" And, of course, there was Max's Deli, home of the egg cream and three-inch thick sandwiches. Oy, what I would give for a pastrami sandwich and knish from Max's, she thought, shaking her head wistfully.

Then she spotted a lone figure in the park, the same old man she saw each day, sitting on a bench wrapped in a coat and muffler. There he is. Right on time. Everyday he sits by himself, she thought. He must be half meshuga to sit alone in the cold like that. She examined his face. From the vantage point of her third-floor window, his face looked kind—the lines etched in his skin were soft and pliable and suggested a lifetime of deep, honest emotion. This is a man capable of friendship. Could such a man not be married? I wish I could see if he is wearing a ring. I wonder if he has a place to go, if he has family? The poor thing, sitting by himself day after day. Thank God there's sun today, at least he can keep warm, she thought.

She looked down at the old man again and studied his hawk-like profile cutting into the light. His long gray hair hung over the collar of his coat and blew in the wind. He looks just a little like father. But what kind of man doesn't wear a hat in this weather? Miss Bargman thought. He will be lucky if he doesn't catch his death. A man such as this needs a wife to look after him, a woman to take care of the little things.

The sun loosened the tightness in the old woman's shoulders, and the dull pain in her back dissolved. She smelled the warm, musty odor of her woolen sweater. I will just sit and rest here for a while. But then she had second thoughts. I should finish cleaning, just in case someone . . . Ach, I've done enough for now. I need to worry the president should come to visit? Rest is more important. Even father took naps, even him. So why do I feel so guilty when I rest? Miss Bargman felt the warmth of the sun wrap around her. Rest is important for someone who is eighty-nine, she thought as she burrowed deeper into the cushion of the chair. God, I never thought I would live this long. Nobody should outlive family and friends.

As the sun began to sap her energy, fatigue overtook her. I should begin preparing dinner. But I'm so tired. Maybe if I close my eyes, just for a moment, no more, then I can finish with my cooking and cleaning . . . Just a short rest, not a nap, just a short rest, Miss Bargman told herself as she leaned her head back and closed her eyes.

It was two o'clock and time for her afternoon tea. She picked up the teakettle, filled it with water, put the lid back on, and placed it on the stove. She reached for the knob to turn on the burner but stopped and thought, I wonder if the old man is still in the park? She walked across the room to the window and saw no one on the bench. Miss Bargman was disappointed. I wonder if he likes to have a cup of tea in the afternoon? Then, feeling her legs weaken beneath her, she said to herself impatiently, I don't know why I bother checking up on the old man. What difference does it make whether he is in the park or if he drinks tea? It won't change the fact that I am an old woman living in a run-down, dying neighborhood. Then Miss Bargman wondered why the kettle hadn't whistled yet. She walked back to the stove and saw that she had not turned on the burner. Ach, I can't even make tea anymore. What good is an old woman if she can't even make tea? The only thing an old woman is good for is dying, she thought bitterly.

More often then ever, Miss Bargman thought about dying. These thoughts usually came to the old woman at night. She would pace the floors of her apartment, consumed by fear and worry. She couldn't stop her mind from racing toward the abyss. Nervous, tense, she would often think, I must get out of this morgue of an apartment. But instead of leaving, she would worry even more.

Is it possible nobody will know when I die, and I'll lie in my apartment for days? Could it happen that even after a day or two nobody will notice I'm not moving around or sitting at my window? These worries haunted the old woman. Her anxiety now interfered with her few enjoyments. I wonder what people will say about me after I'm gone? Will they laugh about the old woman who died in her apartment and nobody found the body for days afterward? Will they gossip—what kind of woman has nobody checking on her? These thoughts terrified the old woman.

Bathed in the warmth of the sunlight, Miss Bargman felt her heart beating rapidly. Her breathing was raspy and shallow, and she felt beads of sweat on her upper lip. The thought of this gossip left her feeling weak and strangely embarrassed. She picked up her teacup, took another sip of tea, and then looked at her watch and saw it was time to plan her evening meal. Enough of the kvetching, you old fool, she told herself. I better get to work, or I will go hungry tonight. After all, bread doesn't come from flour alone.

It was seven o'clock when the old woman finished setting the table for her meal. A quiet, uneventful night had fallen. Flickering lights from the street lamps cast dancing shapes on the walls of her room. At the center of the table was a tall clear glass vase holding three long stem roses. They stood stiffly, soldiers on guard at the Sabbath table. A bowl of apples, oranges, and pears, their skins glowing in the dim light, was at the center of the table. The smell of freshly baked potato kugel filled the air, and a small bowl of matzo ball soup sat on her dinner plate. A golden brown Sabbath loaf lay on a silver tray ready for slicing. Two tall white candles in silver candlesticks loomed over her plate. As Miss Bargman sat surveying her table, she heard the faint tick of the clock marking time in the quiet apartment. She thought of the old man and hoped he had a place to go for a warm meal. No one should be alone, especially an old man, she said to herself, closing her eyes. Life is hard enough without sitting alone at the dinner table.

Miss Bargman looked at all the food she had placed around her table. So much for one person, she thought. Why go to all the trouble when there is no one to share with? Is it extravagant for me to prepare such a meal each Friday just for myself?

Why do I have such thoughts? It's not possible for me to be content for once and enjoy a quiet meal? What did mother used to say? 'Lots of food makes for a festive mood.' And then, she thought, you never know, a visitor could arrive unexpectedly. Desperately hanging on to that hope, the old woman's eyes filled with tears as she began to eat her meal in the solitude of her apartment.

The Sabbath candles burned, and the old woman sat quietly absorbed in her thoughts. Swallowing a yawn, she looked at her empty plate. Her eyelids began to close as she listened to the rhythm of her own shallow breathing. *Why should eating make me so tired? Eighty-nine years of Sabbath meals. How many more years before it's my time?* she wondered. *Oh, how life slips by so fast.* She thought of friends when she was a young girl, their families singing songs after the Sabbath meal, the old passing traditions to the young. *Those were such happy times for me!* Now, the old woman felt like a relic from the past. She didn't belong anymore; her life had become unnecessary and unimportant.

"You silly old woman," she said aloud. *I shouldn't think so foolishly. I must have a positive attitude and look to the future. I have to remind myself of that,* she told herself as she pushed away from the table.

It was ten o'clock when Miss Bargman finished putting away her dishes. She took the wine bottle out of the cabinet to pour a glass as she did each night.

The pop of the cork made her smile.

She listened to the sound of the wine splashing into her glass. Then, silence again. She sat expressionless, her face slack and vulnerable. She was exhausted and felt every bit of her eighty-nine years. In a moment of self-doubt she called out, "Oh God! Is this life worth living, the aches and pains, the tsuris, the loneliness? Does my life have value? God, can you give a sign, anything to let me know if this struggle is worth it, if it matters whether I live or die?"

The old woman sat for a long time and gazed around the room, waiting.

Finally she thought, What if an old friend should call, somebody needing a friendly ear to listen, someone requiring my counsel on matters large or small? What if an old, lonely Jew, someone without friends or family to share a warm, well-prepared meal needs a place at my table? Someone must be there for them. Someone must care enough to provide a warm meal and companionship.

Troubled, she thought, Is that God's plan for me, to sit and wait for someone to call?

She slowly shifted her gaze to the window that overlooked the park. A jolt shook the old woman as she thought of all the years she had spent sitting and waiting for good things to come her way. Everyday I watch the old man from my window and everyday he sits by himself. Immediately she understood what she must do. "Ach, enough of the sitting and waiting," she cried. I've done that my whole life. Yes! When the weather warms I will go to the park and talk to the old man. It's the least I can do for an old, lonely Jew. After all, he is only half-meshuga. And who knows, maybe he hasn't been invited out for some time. I can prepare a meal for him he won't soon forget. Ah, a noodle kugel with apples, raisins, and walnuts—yes, something to get the old man to think just a little about the cook. For me, preparing such a meal will be child's play.

As she raised the glass to close her day, the old woman's eyes danced with excitement. She thought of her mother and father, then of friends no longer with her. Mostly though, she thought of spring, just weeks away, its warm gentle breezes carrying perfumed air and promises of good things to come. Her pulse quickened. Yes, when the weather warms, I will make my introduction. Who knows, maybe the old man is a mensch. Smiling coyly as only an old, lonely woman can, Miss Bargman said in a soft voice, "Yes, it's a foolish thing for me to sit up here and the old man out there in the cold. For isn't it written that a good Jew must take advantage of all the good things God offers?" And then, with great ceremony and élan, she raised her glass high into the air, took a deep breath, and toasted, "L'chaim!"

∾